GWEN GRANT

Private – Keep Out!

Illustrated by Sandra Wright

BARN OWL BOOKS

for Ian

First published in Great Britain 1978
by Heinemann Young Books, Egmont Children's Books
239 Kensington High Street, London WC1A 1NU
This edition first published 1999 by Barn Owl Books
15 New Cavendish Street, London W1M 7RL

ISBN 1 903015 02 2
A CIP catalogue record for this book
is available from the British Library

Designed and typeset by Douglas Martin
Printed and bound in Great Britain by
Cox & Wyman Limited, Reading

PRIVATE – KEEP OUT!

The hilarious adventures of a girl, the youngest of six, growing up in a mining town just after the War. Our heroine, high-spirited, impulsive, stubborn is never out of trouble but always manages to stay lovable.

Contents

Chapter One

'Who said ghosts can see in the dark?'

Well, it's not often a great bundle of clean paper comes my way like this, so I've decided I'm going to use it for writing about the street where I live and then when I'm very old, say about thirty, I'll be able to read all about what happened in 1948. I want to be a writer when I grow up, so this'll be good practice.

I suppose I ought to mention how I came to get hold of all this paper first. Well, now then (that's a thing I'll have to watch – using 'Well' all the time). I think I'm beginning to change my mind about being a writer. It's too fiddly. You've got to worry all the time. Mind you, our Mam worries something terrible and she doesn't write. She cleans the animal ladies' house out three times a week. The animal ladies look after cats and dogs other people don't want. I don't know why they need someone to clean for them. There's only two of them and no kids, as our Mam always says. There's six kids in our family and our Mam has to clean for us all.

First, there's our Mam and Dad, who're all right really. Then, there's our Pete, who's the eldest and works on a farm and thinks he knows everything and says, 'Do this. Do that', all the time. If you even so much as shake your head to say, 'No', he starts going mad and saying 'Do as you're told else you'll get a rattle round the earhole.' It makes you think brothers aren't up to much which isn't very good for me because I've got two more.

There's our Tone, he's the next eldest, and just because he's as big as a house side he thinks he's going to be the champion boxer of the world in two years time when he's eighteen. I said to him, 'You couldn't box your way out of a paper bag,' and I had to lock myself in the lavatory for about fourteen hours till our Mam rescued me.

I haven't written down all the bad news yet because I've also got two sisters. Just writing that makes me sad.

There's our Lucy. She's the next in age to our Tone and she's still at school, but only till Christmas and then she leaves. She combs her hair over one eye like a film star and looks in the mirror a lot. She's got a job in a dress shop and thinks she's the cat's whiskers because of that. 'I don't know about cat's whiskers,' I said to her. 'You look more like a dog's dinner to me,' and she went wild. I said to her, 'If I threw you a piece of meat now, it'd be gone in a flash,' and then I had to run faster than I've ever run before. She told our Mam that unless something was done about me showing her up in front of her mates, she'd do something about me herself.

'Why didn't you stand me on top of a hill when the war

was on?' I said once, because I was fed up to the back teeth with them getting mad at me all the time. That's the biggest trouble with our family. They've none of them got a sense of humour. They can't take a joke, not for any money they can't.

Our Lucy said if she'd known then what she knew now, she would have stood me on top of a hill when the war was on with a big arrow pointing at me, saying, 'shoot here', and they all fell about laughing, so then our Mam rattled them for being so unkind to me and making me cry. I must say that made me laugh all right.

It's writing all this down which makes me realise how unlucky I am, because next there's our Rose. She goes to the same school as me but she always tells everybody she's not really my sister at all. That's because I've got black curly hair and say 'Mam' and she's got blonde curly hair and says 'Mother'. She says our Mam found her on our front doorstep and she's really a princess in disguise and there was this note pinned to her and it said, 'This is a princess in disguise. Look after her and you shall be rewarded'.

I said to our Mam, 'Did you really find her on our front doorstep?' and she said, 'What do you think?' and I said, 'Because if you did, I think you should have left her there.'

'What?' says our Mam. 'Leave a poor little baby in the snow?' and I said, 'This wasn't a poor little baby though. This was our Rose,' and our Mam laughed and said, 'Now, Rose is a very nice girl,' and I looked at her and I thought, 'You can tell she's a Mam thinking our Rose is a nice girl.'

I'm nearly at the end of them now, thank goodness, because all this is making me feel really miserable. Next, there's our Joe. He's all right. He's a big head and thinks he knows everything in the entire world and he goes on and on about aeroplanes and guns and daft things like that but I don't mind him too much. I always liked him better after he showed me how to be a pilot in a Spitfire and he went round the street going 'Bbbbbbrrrrrr!' and spitting pebbles out of his mouth and one went straight through Mrs Elston's front window.

'Who did that? Who did that?' she shouts, rushing out and catching hold of our Joe. 'It was me bullets, Missis,' our Joe said and Mrs Elston said 'What? What? I'll give you bullets, young Joe,' and she gave him a real shaking. All of a sudden our Joe went bright red and went 'Erk!' – gasp, gasp, gasp – and Mrs Elston said 'Whatever's wrong, lad? Whatever's wrong?' and I said to her, 'I think he's swallowed the rest of his bullets,' and Mrs Elston said 'Bullets. Bullets. What bullets?' I told her about the pebbles in our Joe's mouth that were supposed to be bullets and Mrs Elston went, 'Oh! Oh!!' – scream scream – and our Mam rushed out and our Joe was going 'Ugh!' – gasp gasp – 'I'm dying,' and our Mam thumped him sharpish on the back and this great big pebble shot straight out of his throat.

'Look at that,' our Joe said and we all stood and looked at the bullet lying on the floor and our Mam had to be given a cup of tea and so did Mrs Elston and I had to fetch Grannie Bates to make it because neither of them could lift a kettle on account of how their hands were shaking.

'I'll never make old bones,' our Mam said to Mrs Elston, and Mrs Elston said at the rate our family were going, neither would anybody else in the street either.

Anyway, that's all our family, thank goodness.

Now then, where was I? Oh yes, I was going to tell how I got hold of all this paper. Well, me and our Mam went to a jumble sale at the Methodist Chapel Hall and it was underneath a great pile of old rubbish. I could hardly believe my eyes when I saw it.

'Get us this, Mam,' I said, and she turned round and looked down at me staggering around with it in my arms and said, 'Why, you can hardly stand. Whatever will you do with all that paper?'

'I shall write on it,' I promised her.

'Well,' she said, 'if you're sure and you won't waste it?' I nearly fell over backwards telling her I wouldn't waste it.

'All right then,' she nodded. 'But I shall expect to see you writing on that, young lady.'

'Oh, you will,' I said, and so she bought it for me. It was threepence and if this was one of those snooty comics, I'd say, 'And I will have to have it stopped out of my pocket money.' But it isn't and I don't get pocket money either. We can't afford it.

All the boys in the comics I read go away to boarding school. I don't read girls' comics because our Mam can't afford to buy girls and boys comics, so we have to have comics for the lads. I don't mind, though. I'd rather read about Desperate Dan than about posh old Angela and Fenella and Jennifer who do nothing but eat at night when they're supposed to be in bed asleep. Mind you, they don't do anything very much more interesting in the daytime either. They're either playing hockey or riding horses.

Our Rose got hold of one of these comics once and she said to our Mam, 'Can I have a pony ?' and our Mam said, 'Oh yes, I'm sure. You can have three if you ask nice,' and our Rose got all red in the face and started crying.

'This is a rotten old house,' she said. 'You can't have anything in this house,' but of course she was dead wrong, as usual, because our Mam said, 'Oh yes, you can. You can have this,' and she clipped her round the leg for being such a mardy baby. I laughed – like a drain, which I shouldn't have done, because I got a clip as well, for making fun out of other people's misfortunes, as my Mother said (I call her Mother when I don't like her very much).

Well, the idea was to write about where I live, wasn't it?

And you needn't think I haven't noticed that 'Well' at the beginning because I have, but I'm ignoring it.

Our Dad says we live in a market town, because we have a cattle market where they sell sheep and pigs and cows and that, and a market with stalls where they sell everything you can think of. He says it is also a pit town, because there are a lot of pits where the men work. Our Tone works down the pit. So you can see it's a funny town when it's two things at once.

Where I live there are lots of streets, but we really live in about six of them. There's River Street, Bank Street, Shore Street, Willow Terrace, Avon Place and the Black Hole of Calcutta which is really called End Street. We live in River Street and it's the nicest street of the lot. There are sixteen houses in River Street. Eight down each side. There are some pretty horrible kids who live round here, not including me, of course. I'm nice (ha, ha). I never thought of that. I can write all nice things about myself.

It's not posh where we live. All the rest of the town is posh but we're not. There's a school just round the corner where we all go and there's a big sand quarry where we play, although you're not supposed to. They keep a man with a big black dog in the sand quarry and every now and again he chases you and for about a day after you go around saying 'I'm never going in that quarry again,' but then you forget and you do.

The streets are all twisty and they've got passages and entries in them that lead through to other streets. When anybody chases you, if you know your way around, you can get away from them easy by using the entries and passages. There are hundreds and hundreds of people living in the streets around here, and in summer each street has a big party and that's the only time everybody's friends with everybody else.

There are some little shops and about three pubs and a long road which leads to the bluebell wood and the fields. We spend a lot of time in the fields and the woods in the summer.

I told our Lucy I'm going to be a writer when I grow up and she said, 'You should be a good one then. You tell enough lies.'

Then I told her how much I hated her and she hit me and I said, 'When I'm big, I'm going to hit you and hit you,' and she said, 'When you're big enough, you'll be too old. Anyway, what will you hit me with? Your walking stick?' and then she fell about laughing. There are times when I wish I was an only child.

Of course, it's a week since I last wrote anything in here. I wasn't sure about being a writer but our Mam sort of decided it for me because she said, 'Where's all that paper I bought you?' and I said, 'Upstairs,' and she said, 'Not doing a lot of good up there, is it? 'Then she stared at me in that particular way I hate because it always means she's going to say something like, 'And when did you last wash your face?' and she said, 'I'd better see you writing on that paper, my lass, when I get back, or you'll hear all about it.'

'I can't think of anything to write,' I said, and our Joe, who just happened to be sat imitating a sack of potatoes, said, 'You want to write down some of them lies you tell at school then. I should think they'll fill up three-quarters of it without any bother.'

'What lies?' I shouted, noticing our Mam was giving her impression of Sherlock Holmes. 'I don't tell no lies,' I said, and then our Mam said, 'Well, you'll not go far if you use grammar like that and that's a fact,' and in the end, I left them to it and swept out of the room.

I read that in a book once. 'She swept out of the room,' it said, and I've wanted to do it ever since. Mind you, it would have been a lot better if our Joe hadn't got his great foot in the way.

I've been seriously thinking of going to live on a desert island for a bit of peace because if I didn't know my own brothers personally, I wouldn't believe such a horrible bunch could exist and they make me sick.

The other night I went to bed as usual at about half-past nine. It was pitch black, and we don't have electricity in our house. It hasn't come up into our streets yet. I heard this man on the wireless the other day saying all the world would have electricity by 1980, so we've only got thirty-two years to go. They've got it at school. Well, they would, wouldn't they? But we haven't got it.

'What you never had, you never miss,' our Mam says, but I don't think she's right. I miss a lot of things I've never had, not least of which is a bike. If I had a bike, I should think I'd never ask for anything else in the world again, but our Mam says, 'Oh yes, you would. It's in human nature to want one thing and then another.'

'I'm different, Mam,' I said. 'You buy me a bike and I'll show you.'

'I'll just have to take your word for it,' she said. 'Because you're getting no bike.'

I never expected to get one anyway, but I'm just proving that you can miss what you've never had, even if our Mam doesn't believe it.

So, as I was saying. I went to bed at about half-past nine and somebody shut the stairs door at the bottom so that I couldn't see where I was going, naturally. I was only halfway upstairs and it was really spooky. We have to have a candle with us because there's no gas upstairs either. Only downstairs in the kitchen and the front room. So there I was, halfway upstairs with a candle in my hand and I thought, ooooh! I don't like this, and I nearly went back down.

Anyway, I got into my bedroom all right. Well, it isn't *my* bedroom. I share it with our Mam and Dad, Lucy and Rose. Me, Lucy and Rose sleep in one bed and our Mam and Dad sleep in another. It's all right, but it gets a bit crowded at times.

Because I'm the youngest, I have to go to bed first, which I think is dead unfair. So I put the candle on the table at the side of the bed and I got into bed and I have to sleep in the middle and you should just try that. It's terrible. I get up every morning black and blue with people's arms hitting me in the face and great big feet kicking me in the back and then our Lucy and Rose turning over at the same time. I know what it's like to be a sardine in a tin, I do. And I wish our Lucy and Rose had tails. Then I wouldn't have to keep on at them about cutting their toe-nails.

Where was I ? Oh yes. So I got into bed and I'd just laid down and the bedroom door started opening very slowly. It went, 'Cccccccrrrrrreeeeeaaaaakkkkk – ccrrreee-aaakkkk.' I nearly died there and then and I felt just like our Dad says a rabbit behaves when it's faced with a fox. I couldn't move. I just sat there bolt up-right and the candle was making all flickering shadows in the room, and because the door was half open the curtains were blowing out. And then, this candle appeared at the end of a long white arm and there was this horrible wailing noise. 'Oooooooohhhhhhhhh!' it went, and then again, 'Ooooooooohhhhhhhhh!' And from behind the door came a ghost! Holding a candle!

Of course I screamed and screamed and screamed and three-quarters of the neighbourhood rushed up the stairs to see what was wrong.

There was my Mam and my Dad and Mrs Elston from next door, and Granny Bates from across the road and Old Flo from round the corner. What a crush! I can just remember seeing Old Flo and Granny Bates sticking in the doorway.

'Get out of the way, Flo,' Granny Bates said and Flo said, 'I'm sure I shan't. I've as much right here as you have,' and our Mam said to our Dad, 'For goodness sake, give them a push so that one or the other of them gets in.' And he did and they came out of the door with a pop, like a cork out of a bottle.

'Whatever's the matter?' our Mam was shouting at me, and Granny Bates leant over me and said, 'That child's not well,' and our Mam said, 'Go on!' and Granny Bates said, 'Oh well, if that's the attitude you're going to take,' but she didn't go away.

Then Old Flo looked at me and said, 'Do you remember when old Johnny Boy was taken away?' I remember when he was taken away because he was shouting and screaming at the end of our street and our Mam said it was because he was shell-shocked in the war. That means somebody dropped a bomb on him and it hurt him in his head, in the bit where you think. I stopped screaming and gulped and yelled at our Mam, 'Don't let them take me away,' and our Mam lifted me out of bed and said to Old Flo, 'You'd better go down, Flo. I'll see to her,' and our Dad got them all back downstairs.

'What's wrong?' our Mam said and I told her about the ghost and she said, 'And it was carrying a candle, was it?' and I sobbed, 'Yes, Mam, it was,' and she said, 'That's very interesting,' and she laid me down again and said, 'Dad'll bring you a nice cup of cocoa in a minute. You just lie there.'

'But what about the ghost?' I yelled and she said, 'Oh, I don't think that'll bother you any more,' and she shouted to our Lucy and told her to sit with me, and our Lucy moaned and groaned and said, 'Rotten little thing,' and our Mam heard her and rattled her one. So then, of course, our Lucy rattled me as soon as our Mam had gone out of the room.

I thought a bomb had dropped on our house because I heard our lads shrieking and yelling and our Mam shouting and carrying on and yes, you've got it, it was them, wasn't it? Our Joe sat on Tone's shoulders with a sheet over his head, which fell right to the floor, while our Pete held the candle and opened the door for them. They think they're so funny. I'll probably never forgive them till the day I die, but as I can't see me lasting very long in this madhouse, I don't suppose it matters very much.

Chapter Two

'What are angels, Mam?'

None of our lads are speaking to me because of last night and every time our Joe comes anywhere near me, he pinches me as hard as he can.

'I'll tell our Mam,' I says to him and he starts shouting, 'Tell tale tit, you're a skinny nit, and I'm going to bash you with a walking stick.' So I kicked him and he went hobbling round shouting 'Oooh! Oooh!' and our Mam comes rushing into the kitchen and she says, 'If there's any more bother with you two, I'll take a hand,' and I says, 'It's all his fault, Mam,' and our Joe says, 'Look at my leg. Look what she's done to it.'

Then he shows our Mam the place where he fell down this morning and skinned it and our Mam looks at his leg and says to me, 'Right, madam,' and before I can move, slaps me sharply on the arm. So I go, 'Oh! Oh! The pain! The pain!' and our Mam says to us both, 'If you're not out of here in five seconds flat, you'll both go to bed for the rest of the day.' So we got out.

When we were outside, I said to our Joe, 'Don't think you've got away with anything because you haven't. I'll get even with you and our Pete and Tone if it's the last thing I do,' and our Joe says, 'You try anything and it will be,' and I said, 'You can't scare me,' and wondered if my guardian angel would hang around and see I was all right. Everybody's supposed to have a guardian angel. At least, that's what they tell us at Sunday School. I'm not saying I don't believe them because if I didn't have one, I'd be in about a million little pieces by now with our lot. All I'm saying is that mine must have the longest dinner hours in history because every time I get into bother, it's never there.

I said to our Mam once, 'Are angels men or women?' and she went, 'Oh! Ah! Yes, well,' and I looked at her and she looked at me and I thought, that's not told me very much. So I said, 'Are they, Mam?' and she said, 'I'm not sure,' and I said to her, 'They all wear nightgowns,' and she said, 'I don't think they're nightgowns they wear,' and I said to her, 'What are they then?' and she said, 'Robes.' I said, 'Well, they look like nightgowns,' and she said, 'Do you think I've got all day to stand here talking about what angels wear?' And I thought, 'So! Our Mam doesn't know whether they're men or women either,' and I thought, I must remember to ask at Sunday School.

When I asked, the teacher went, 'Good gracious me!' and looked as if he were going to faint clean away. 'What a question to ask,' he says. 'They're just angels,' which as far as I'm concerned is the very worst answer to a question I've ever heard and which only goes to show that no grown-ups ever tell anybody smaller than themselves that they don't know the answer. I expect our Sunday School teacher will get to go to heaven seeing as he already sort of works for them, but I can't see him in a nightgown.

I said to our Mam, 'Do you think haloes are on sticks?'

and she said, 'Whatever did I do to deserve you?' and I said to her, 'Well, if they're not on sticks on your back, how do they move at the same time as the angels move?' Our Joe says, 'They're like magnets,' and I said, 'Don't be daft. How can they be like magnets? Angels haven't got iron heads,' and he said, 'Well, you'll never get to be one then, will you, because your head's solid iron all the way through,' and, of course, he thought that was very funny.

I find angels very puzzling.

Our Joe thinks I'll forget about them being ghosts but I'll get even with them.

Anyway, we all went down to the sand quarry today. All the big lads were there as well with it being a Saturday afternoon. They were all hammering and sawing and banging away at these pieces of wood they'd got from the wood-yard so I went over and says to our Joe, 'What are you doing?' and he says, 'Wouldn't you like to know?' and I says, 'Yes, that's why I'm asking;' and he says, 'Mind your own business,' so I went and laid on top of one of the cliffs and watched them for a bit.

They were nailing all the little pieces to the big pieces and then when they'd finished they were laying them side by side and joining them together. I could see then they were making a raft.

Anyway, when they'd got all these pieces of wood nailed together, they fetched four empty tin drums from the pile the old watchman kept near his shed and they laid the raft on top of these drums and started tying them on with rope.

Our Pete shouts to one of the lads, 'I don't think we've got enough rope to make sure these drums stop on. Shall we fetch some more just to be on the safe side?' Then all these lads go mutter, mutter, yers, yers, and so they all decide to go and see if the wood-yard man has any spare pieces of rope they can borrow. They went off and left one little lad on guard over this stupid raft they'd made.

I went down the cliff and I says to this little lad, 'Do you want a sweet?' and he says, 'Why?' and I says, 'Oh, never mind, never mind. If you don't want one, it doesn't worry me.' He stood there, and then he says, 'What kind?' and I says, 'Caramel,' and he says, 'What I got to do for it?' I says, 'Climb that cliff,' and he says, 'Cor blimey, that's nothing.' I says, 'That's what you say, but what do you do?' and he says, 'Where's the caramel first then?' and I showed it to him, my very last caramel, and he says, 'All right,' and he went running across the sand to the cliffs.

I looked down at the empty tin drums under the raft and carefully unscrewed all the caps and put them in my pocket. Then the little lad comes back and he says, 'There you are. Told you it was easy,' and I gave him the caramel and went back and laid on the cliff top again and all the lads came running into the quarry and wrapped about three hundred feet of rope round their stupid raft and I wondered if any of them would notice that none of the tin drums had their caps on. And they didn't.

I heard our Tone shout, 'Right! Ready to launch! 'Boy, they certainly make me sick, thinking they're admirals or something. Then they all moved the raft into the pond and climbed on board.

Our Pete was standing there with a long bit of wood and he was paddling away as if they were in the middle of the Atlantic Ocean and then I heard our Joe shout, 'We're sinking!' and I could see all white bubbles on top of the pond from where the water was filling the empty drums and the raft was sinking lower and lower.

Our Pete was still paddling away though and he was shouting, 'Get it back to the bank! Get it back to the bank!' and all the lads started paddling with their hands. Then our stupid Tone stands up and starts saluting this little scruffy bit of a flag they had flying from a brush handle they'd stuck in the middle of the raft, just like shipwrecked sailors do on the pictures, and then our Joe stands up and salutes and then our Pete and all the other lads, one after the other. That was the last I saw of them, them standing up saluting as the raft slowly sank to the bottom of the pond. When I left, they were up to their waists already. Boys certainly are stupid. I thought I'd fall off the cliff laughing.

I ran all the way home because I didn't want to miss what happened when they all trailed in wet through and our Mam saw them.

Anyway, when they were dried out and our Mam could speak again, she says, 'Well, what happened?' and our Joe says, 'I don't know. We haven't got the raft out of the pond yet. Must have been an engineering fault,' and our Pete says, 'Can't think what happened.'

Then our Tone looked at me and he says, 'What's so funny?' and I said, 'Funny? Funny? There's nothing funny,' and he went all suspicious looking and said, 'Well, what you laughing at then?' and I says, 'I'm not laughing,' and he says, 'Yes, you are,' and our Pete says, 'Oh, leave her alone. We've got enough trouble without her as well,' and when they weren't looking, I laid all the four drum caps on the tablecloth and went and sat on our Mam's knee.

'What's this in aid of?' she says and then our Joe sees the caps on the table and he says to our Pete and Tone, 'Don't look now,' and they all follow his finger which is shaking because our Joe's got a terrible temper. Then they all look at me and our Joe says, 'I'll kill her,' and our Mam says, 'Here, here. That'll be enough of that kind of talk.' Our Pete says, 'You little devil,' and our Tone says, 'I told you. I knew she was at the bottom of this,' and I said, 'I liked that bit where you saluted best.'

Our Mam looked at the caps and at our lads and then at me and she started laughing so hard she couldn't stop and our Pete says to her, 'I don't know about engineering fault. She's one great big fault,' and I was grinning that much my face hurt. I says to them, 'Mind you don't catch your chins on the floor,' and our Mam stopped laughing and said, 'I shouldn't push your luck, madam. You've got to get off my knee sometime.' So I didn't say anything else but all the same, I do think this must be one of the happiest days of my life.

Chapter Three

'Do I have to go to dancing class?'

I THOUGHT THINGS were going too well to last. We've been rehearsing for this concert at my dancing class and last night I was a little Dutch girl. I can hardly believe it myself. I nearly died when I saw the costume they expected me to wear and our Mam and the dancing teacher had to hold me down while they put it on me. It was horrible.

Our Mam went bright red and the dancing teacher, Fancy Nancy I call her, though her real name is Miss Nancy, kept saying, 'I don't know what's got into you, I really don't,' and I was shouting, 'I'm not putting them frilly knickers on,' and our Mam said, 'I can't see what all the fuss is about. I'm ashamed of you, I am.' And in the end I had to put them on, and our Mam said I must have torn the elastic or something with all my mucking about because they fell down when I was on the stage. 'Serves you right,' our Mam said, 'for making such a song and dance about nothing.'

All I know is that I wished I were dead because everybody shouted and cheered when I picked them up and Miss Nancy's hand came out from behind the curtain and dragged me off the stage. I says to her, 'Look at these red marks you've made round my arm,' and she said, 'It's a pity it was only your arm,' and I thought, oh yes, very nice I'm sure. Miss Nancy has her dancing lessons in the front room of their house. She sells shoes in the daytime down the town. I know because I've seen her in the shop. She never speaks to me though, not even when I stand looking at her through the window. Our Mam says it's a good job the lessons don't cost very much because otherwise I couldn't go. I said to Fancy Nancy, 'You ought to put your prices up,' and she said, 'If I put my prices up, no one would be able to afford to come,' and she didn't put them up. I didn't think she would, but it was worth a try.

Anyway, we learn tap dancing and ballet and acrobatics at dancing class, and twice a year, in the summer and at Christmas, Miss Nancy takes the Church Hall for two nights and we have a concert. That's to show the Mams and Dads how brilliant we all are, but everybody else comes as well. Our Mam says she wouldn't miss one for anything. They all say it makes a nice change, but I bet they wouldn't think so if they were up on that stage with everybody staring at them.

There's this lad who goes to dancing class as well. He was a little Dutch boy in the concert and we had to sing and dance together round this stupid well. It had a handle on it and I was supposed to turn it and a bucket came up. This lad's called James.

Fancy Nancy kept saying to him, 'Naow, James,' (she talks like that when she talks to James. When she talks to me she just says, 'Get a move on, will you?') Anyway, she says, 'Naow, James. Would you move your foot a little to one side, dear? That's right. Oh, that's beautiful, that is.' And James smirks and flutters his eyelashes at her and so, last night, after my knickers fell down, I turned the handle on that stupid well and took the bucket off it like I'd been told and dropped it on dear James's beautiful foot.

You should have heard him yell. And then the horrible thing went on dancing with his teeth grinning at everybody like somebody not right. Of course everybody in the audience clapped and cheered him, so when he took a bow at the end of the dance, I pinched his bottom. That stopped his grinning.

After the curtains came down, he chased me right round the stage and I could hear somebody in the audience saying, 'I wish they'd put that curtain up,' and dear James's mother came round the back and got hold of one of my ears and said, 'I saw you, you nasty little girl, pinching our James like that,' and she started shaking me. Then our Mam came and she said, 'You'd better let go of her,' and dear James's mother said, 'And who might you be, my good woman?' And as 'my good woman' was our Mam, she pushed dear James's mother out of the way and dragged me down the stairs.

She said, 'I'll keep you in bed for a week, you little devil, showing me up like that,' and I stood there scowling at my shoes. I didn't dare scowl at our Mam because she was as mad as a wet hen. She looked at me and then she started shaking her head and saying, 'I don't know where you're going to end up, madam, I really don't.'

'Well,' I said, 'dear James laughed when my knickers fell down, Mam.'

'If you'd put them knickers on properly when you got dressed in the first place,' our Mam said, 'they wouldn't have fallen down at all. I don't know how you're going to live that down, I don't.'

And I don't either. Luckily, it's not school for another

week, so perhaps everybody will have forgotten by then. Anyway, our Mam has put some elastic in them knickers about three feet wide it is and when I put them on, I thought my top half was going to fall off. 'They're a bit tight, Mam,' I said, and she said, 'I should just think they are a bit tight after that carry on last night.'

'I can't breathe,' I said. And she said, 'What do you want to breathe for? If them knickers fall down again, you'd be better off not breathing anyway, so just keep quiet and let me finish them.'

I expect I shall go on the stage tonight and when I lean over I shall fall off my waist. Nobody'll care, I know that.

I says to our Mam, 'Why do I have to be a little Dutch girl?' and she says, 'Into every life a little rain must fall,' and I looked at her and said, 'But, Mam, my life is soaking wet through already,' and she said, 'And it'll get even wetter, madam, if you don't behave yourself tonight with that little boy.' I said 'Little boy! Do you mean James?' and she said yes, that was exactly who she did mean and I said, 'He's not a little boy, Mam. He's a monkey in disguise,' and our Mam said to watch my tongue else I might find it being washed with soap and water before I was finished so I kept quiet and didn't say anything else, but I thought a lot.

When we got to the Church Hall though, Fancy Nancy wouldn't let me be a little Dutch girl again. I was really glad. I hate that dear James more than anybody in the world, and when you reckon that includes our Pete and Tone and Joe and Lucy and Rose, you can see just how much I hate him.

Our Mam was ever so mad about it and she said to Fancy Nancy, 'I shan't let her come again, you know,' and Fancy Nancy said, 'That, Mrs Hall, would be a blessing undisguised,' whatever that might mean. Anyway, in the end, she said, 'She can be a fairy if she wants to be, but I'm not having any more trouble like last night. Poor dear James can hardly walk today on that foot, and he has a bruise on his bottom the size of a teacup where your daughter pinched him.'

'She won't do it again,' our Mam said, 'will you?' staring at me as if she were a teacher.

'No,' I said. 'I shan't do it again.'

So, Miss Nancy said, 'Very well then, she can be a fairy,' and all I can say is that when I grow up, I shall burn every single book about fairies I can get my hands on.

They always have to have wings, you know, and they're made out of silver paper and stuff and if you move an inch, somebody shouts at you, 'Mind your wings.' I tried them out tonight before the concert. I jumped off the beam over the stage and flapped them as fast as I could but nothing happened. I only flattened another fairy I fell on who was practising her steps. They try and stuff you up with anything, these books and grown-ups between them.

Our Lucy said after, 'You knew you wouldn't fly, you daft thing. What did you have to go and jump for? That poor little girl you landed on is black and blue. You wait till our Mam gets hold of you.' But I was past caring by then. The only thing was, I bent my magic wand and I had to go on the stage with it crooked.

Luckily, when the star fell off, it fell on dear James's head, so the night wasn't a complete waste after all.

Miss Nancy was sat crying when we came off. She stood up when I passed her and she said, 'If ever I see you again, I shall not be responsible for my actions,' and I said, 'Well, I never wanted to be a fairy in the first place,' and then our Mam came up and she just looked at me and said, 'Home, young lady. You and me have got some talking to do.' So now I'm in trouble every which way.

The only thing I know is that I hate dear James, Fancy Nancy and fairies. And as for little Dutch girls, if they wear knickers with as much elastic in them as mine had, I feel sorry for them, that's all.

Anyway, I couldn't go back to Fancy Nancy because she wouldn't have me. 'I'm surprised you can afford to pick and choose,' our Mam said to her, and Fancy Nancy said, 'I'd rather sweep roads than teach *her* any more,' and our Mam said, 'If that's the way you feel, there's no more to be said.'

I said to our Mam, 'What shall I do now Miss Nancy won't have me?' and our Mam said, 'I suppose we shall have to try and get some other poor soul to take you on.' Sometimes I don't think our Mam is altogether on my side.

So she took me to this new teacher, Miss Brown. Ruby Brown her name is. I said to her, 'That's a funny name,' and she said, 'Why? I don't think it's funny,' and I said, 'Well, rubies are red, not brown,' and she sighed and said, 'Who was your last teacher?' and when I said, 'Fancy Nancy . . . er, sorry, Miss Nancy,' she looked at me and said, 'I hope you're going to behave yourself,' and I said of course I was.

Miss Brown is tall and thin with brown curly hair and she works in the same shop as our Lucy's going to work at. She sells frocks. She'll be in charge of our Lucy, who I feel very sorry for. I wouldn't like to work with Miss Brown. I don't even want to go to her dancing class, but our Mam says I've got to, so that's that. Miss Brown always seems to be looking at you, just like a proper teacher. She doesn't have her lessons in her Mam's front room. She has a room over the wallpaper shop for her lessons. It's freezing in there as well, but our Mam says at the prices she charges she can't afford to have it heated. One thing with Miss Brown, you have to dance, because if you stood still for a second you'd get that cold you'd never move again.

So, we started. By the time we'd finished I could hardly move. I'm sure Miss Brown thinks all my bones are sewn together in a lot of little bits and pieces instead of being all in one line. She kept saying, 'Now, bend it here,' and wanting me to bend one of those bits of my legs that don't bend. I said to her, 'They don't bend, ' and she said, 'They will by the time I've finished.'

When I went to dancing class tonight, Miss Brown said she wanted me to pretend I was a leaf and float about in the air and everything. So I did for about fourteen hours and then I laid down on the floor and she came up and said to me, 'And what do you think you're doing?' and I said, 'I'm being a leaf, ' and she said, 'You don't look much like a leaf to me. To me, you look as if you're just lying on the floor,' and I said, 'Well, I'm lying on the floor because I've just fallen off a tree,' and she said, 'Get up! Get up, you horrible little child, ' and I thought, huh!

So then I had to be a tree and I shouted, 'TIMBER,' and fell down and bashed a lot of little leaves who were *still* floating about in the air, and they all started crying.

Miss Brown nearly went mad. She got hold of me and I was glad it was only my wrist and not my neck she had in her hands and she said, 'If you cannot behave yourself, child, then I shall have to tell your mother that I will not have you in my class. Not at all. Do you understand?' I said, 'Right, Miss. Sorry, Miss,' and she said, 'Right. Now go and be a river. You surely can't get up to any harm being a river,' and I said, 'But you said be a tree, Miss,' and she said, 'Just *go away*,' and so I went and started being a river.

I had to lay on the floor and roll about pretending to be moving and that. That was pretty horrible and I was glad to get home. Then I got into trouble because our Mam took one look at me and she said, 'And what have you been doing in those clothes?' and I said, 'I've been being a river,' and she went, 'Tut, tut! I don't know. I suppose you were a dirty river, were you?' and started laughing. But I didn't think it was funny at all.

Chapter Four

'Why are there spots on my face?'

I KNOW I WAS DIRTY when I got home from dancing class last night, thanks to Miss Brown, who I don't think I'm going to like very much and who I don't think is going to like me very much either, but when I got up this morning and looked in the mirror I thought, that's funny, I don't look very clean, and I knew I couldn't be that dirty because we always have to have a wash at night before we go to bed. I know I didn't exactly have a wash last night but I splashed some water on my face and I thought, I shouldn't look brown.

Anyway, I had another wash and that isn't like me at all. In fact, our Mam shouted through to the kitchen, 'You're never actually getting washed, are you?' and I said, 'I won't come clean, Mam.' She said, 'Don't be daft. Get a move on else you'll be late for school,' although why that should bother anybody I don't know. Personally, I couldn't care if I was so late for school it was finished for the day by the time I got there, but still.

Anyway, in the end, our Mam came into the kitchen and she took one look at me and went, 'Aaaagh!' (just like in the comics) and said, 'You're covered in spots,' and I thought, oh, I don't feel very well, although I'd felt all right up till then. Of course, nothing would suit but that our Lucy and Rose came rushing in. 'Spotty! Spotty!' they started shouting and I burst into tears. Just like that, and then the nicest thing that ever happened to me in my life happened then. Our Mam clouted them for making me cry when I was poorly. It was worth every spot I ever had and I'm not kidding. Anyway, I said, 'I don't feel very well,' and our Mam said, 'Come on, let's have you back to bed.' I'd just settled down and was reading all the comics which had only come that very morning (I don't usually get to see them till all the big ones have read them, and by that time they're practically in tatters) when Old Flo came up the stairs.

I can say here and now that if I'd known our Mam was going to call Old Flo in, I'd have pasted my face with flour like our Lucy does when she goes out at night and thinks our Mam hasn't seen her. She looks just like a ghost although she thinks she looks beautiful. I would have done anything rather than let our Mam see my spots if I'd known she was going to have Old Flo in.

Anyway, Old Flo leant over me and that practically gave me double chicken pox in itself because she leans over you and breathes all over you and makes you feel ill and then she prods and pokes at you until you feel like a pin cushion. She has these long thin fingers and it doesn't half hurt when she sticks them in you.

'Ho yes,' she says. 'Definitely chicken spots,' and I thought, oh, ugh! because they don't last as long as some of the other spotty things you get and you have to get up sooner as well.

'No need to get the doctor in,' Old Flo says. 'Get her up in the morning and let her lay on the sofa. Give her plenty to drink and don't worry if she won't eat for a day or two,' and I stared at Flo and thought, what are you trying to do? Ruin everything? The whole world and everything? Because when anyone's ill at our house, they get treated like a queen – or a king if you're a boy, of course.

You get fruit for a start. Now, that's something we never normally see at all, only in the shop windows, that is. Then, you get extra comics and everybody in the street sends round a sweet or an old comic or something. Everybody comes to see you as well and best of all, for all the time you're poorly nobody gets to hit you. None of our lads or Rose and Lucy, that is. Not even any of the kids in the street are supposed to hit you when you're poorly and if they do, your brothers and sisters hit them, which is just about the only time brothers and sisters are of any use at all.

And here was Old Flo, telling our Mam all these lies about how I wasn't hardly poorly at all. I thought, I'm not having this, so I laid back and went, 'Ooooooooooo-hhhhhhhhh. Ooooooooo-hhhhhhhhh. I feel terrible,' and our Mam went white and said, 'Oh, Flo,' and Flo looked at me and said, 'Castor oil. That's what she wants. Castor oil,' and then I saw her wink at our Mam and our Mam said, 'Right then,' and I had to have a great big spoon of castor oil. I did feel ill then, properly.

Some grown-ups spoil the whole world, they do.

Anyway, it was all right for most of the day and then something really terrible happened and I was frightened half out of my life. The rent man called.

Our Mam locked all the doors (there's only two of them but she locked them both) and she drew the curtains and she said, 'Now, you be very quiet, because the rent man's coming and I haven't got the money to pay him today,' and

I felt all shaky inside and scared. I said, 'What'll happen if you don't pay the rent, Mam?' and she said, 'Oh, nothing will happen,' but I knew it would.

The women talk about it all the time and sometimes when you get up in the morning, a whole family will have gone away. They call this a moonlight flit because they go in the dead of night when there's nobody around to see them. My Mam always says, 'Those poor people. No roof over their heads and them with all those little kids as well,' and it's always been a very scary thing for me, that one night I would wake up and be put on a barrow and wheeled away and we'd have no roof over our heads either.

So, we were sat there and I hardly dared breathe at all. In fact, I could feel my face getting redder and redder and our Mam suddenly said, 'Here. You're not to stop breathing altogether, you daft thing,' and slapped me on the back and I was going, 'Ugh! Ugh! Ugh!' and everything because then I couldn't get my breath. Our Mam said, 'I don't know whatever I'm going to do with you. You always take things to extremes,' and she shook her head and then suddenly went dead still and I did too. I was scared half to death.

'Is that him?' I said, and our Mam went, 'Ssshhhh!' I fell back on the cushions and wondered what our lads and Rose and Lucy and our Dad would do when they got home and found they hadn't a roof over their heads any more.

The rent man knocked on the door and everything went quiet. And then I heard him shout to Mrs Elston, 'Is Missis in?' and Mrs Elston said, 'No. She's gone shopping,' and the rent man said, 'That's a likely story, I don't think,' and he started banging and thumping on the door ever so hard. I was nearly dying inside. My heart was going like mad and I said to our Mam, 'Mam, I think my heart's going to burst,' and she just hugged me and put a finger over my lips.

'I know you're in there,' this man was shouting. 'Open this

door. I want my rent,' and then I heard our Dad's voice, 'And you shall have it, fellow-me-lad,' he said and then the next thing we heard was all this shouting as the rent man ran down the passage at the side of our house and then I started crying and then I think I was really ill because they had to get the proper doctor in.

He was very nice and felt my forehead, and his hands were all cool. He was talking very quiet to our Mam and she was standing twisting her apron in her fingers. Then everything went black and I was poorly for a long time.

The only good thing about me being ill was that I got to sleep in a bed of my own. I don't know where our Lucy and Rose slept but all the time I was poorly, I slept in that big bed all on my own. Our Mam slept with me some of the time. She said this morning, 'Well, I never thought I'd ever wish you were getting up to mischief again.'

Of course, when I did get in bother this afternoon and I reminded her of that, she just said, 'I ought to have known better then, didn't I?' and she slapped my legs just as hard as she ever used to. 'I thought I was poorly?' I said and she said, 'You were, but I can see that you're all better now.'

'Is that us back to normal, then?' I asked her and she said, 'Yes, I'm sorry to say it is.'

All I did this afternoon was try on our Lucy's best frock.

You should have heard her when she came upstairs. 'Oh!' – scream, scream – 'I'm going out in that tonight' – scream, scream – 'I do think, Mother,' (Mother! You can tell she's leaving school soon, can't you?) 'I do think Mother, that you could keep this horrible monster from wearing my clothes.' And our Mam came upstairs and looked at the tiny, tiny little tear in the hem of the skirt where I'd accidentally trodden on it, and I'm not kidding, you would have needed a magnifying glass to see it. She said, 'You leave our Lucy's clothes alone now,' and I said, 'But I was only trying it on,' and our Mam says, 'Never mind. Just you leave them alone.' Then our Lucy said, 'Anyway, I want you to go to the shop for me,' and I said, 'What did your last slave die of?' and our Mam went gasp, gasp, and put her hand over her mouth and rushed out of the room. I said to our Lucy, 'See. You've even made our Mam sick.' 'I have not,' our Lucy said. 'She was laughing, and I'm sure I don't know what there is to laugh about,' and she hit me. I started bawling and our Mam shouted up the stairs, 'For goodness sake, you two, pack it in. I should have thought you'd more sense, our Lucy, than to make a little girl cry,' and our Lucy said, 'I'll murder you one of these days, I'm not kidding.'

So I went rushing down the stairs and said to our Mam, 'Our Lucy says she's going to murder me,' and then our Lucy didn't half get a telling off. Oh, I really enjoyed that! So why it was me that got sent to bed early, I don't know. There's no justice in this world, at all, ever.

I says to our Mam, 'Why have I got to go to bed?' and she says, 'Because you've caused enough trouble in one day to last me for a year and because I want some peace and quiet.' And what gets me is that I don't even do anything in the first place. It's all their fault but I get the blame.

So, anyway, I'm lying here writing this and the candle's flickering like mad and I think I'll pack away now and have a puppet show on the wall.

I'd only just started my puppet show when our Rose came upstairs to get ready to go out. She has to do everything our Lucy does. She's getting to stay out pretty late these days too. I think so, anyway. So she put this skirt on. It was a black taffeta skirt. I say 'was' because it isn't any more. She was standing there holding it at the waist and she started twirling round. Round and round she went and the skirt flared right out and the flame on the candle caught it and there was a nasty little sound like a mad pussy cat spitting.

Then our Rose was standing in the middle of a sheet of flame.

I never even thought about what to do. I remembered a film I'd seen at the pictures where this man wrapped a rug around this woman who was on fire, so I jumped out of bed and grabbed our Mam's patchwork quilt and threw it round our Rose. I could see her face in the light of the fire and she had her mouth open as if she was shouting but I couldn't-hear anything at all. Not a single sound. The quilt covered all our Rose's skirt and they fell on the floor and I jumped up and down on them to make sure the fire was right out.

Then our Rose must have found her voice, which didn't surprise me, because I've never known her be quiet for so long at a time, and she started screaming blue murder. Everybody rushed upstairs and our Mam and Dad are in the doorway staring at our Rose standing there with thick black smoke rising up all round her.

She wasn't hurt at all, though, because she hadn't fastened the skirt so when I threw the quilt around it, it dropped straight to the floor. Anyway, we all had another jump on the quilt, and our Mam said, 'Shush, shush,' to our Rose. Our Rose stopped screaming which pleased everybody for about six streets around and our Mam said to her, 'Are you hurt?' and our Rose said, 'No,' and then our Mam dropped in a big heap on the floor. Our Dad sighed and said, 'If ever a man suffered!' and picked her up and laid her on the bed and brushed her hair back from her face and said, 'There, there, my little love,' and slushy things like that. Then our Rose and Lucy said they'd see to her, and they fetched Mrs Elston from next door and she brought some smelling salts and Granny Bates and, of course, Old Flo, and between them they got our Mam sat up on the bed and then she burst into tears and I started crying, because I always do when our Mam cries. Then – yuk, yuk, yuk – our Rose threw her arms round me and said, 'Oh, you brave little girl,' and then she told everybody what I'd done and I was trying to get away from her. 'Gerrof me,' I said at last and she dropped me as if I were a slug crept out from under a stone.

'You might be brave,' she said, 'but you're horrible,' and I said, 'Oh yes, very nice. Save you from a fiery death and that's all the thanks I get,' and our Rose bit her fingernails and looked at me as if she'd like to strangle me.

Anyway, it all ended very nicely for everyone but me, I should like to add. Our Dad took our Mam for a drink and Mrs Elston and Granny Bates and Old Flo thought they might as well go too, seeing as how they'd had such a terrible shock. Our Rose and Lucy went out and that left me still in bed with our Pete and Tone downstairs. I don't reckon much to that at all and I still don't see why I couldn't go for a nice drink because after all, I had a shock as well, didn't I?

All our Dad would say when I asked if I could go was that his last wish on earth would be that every man and woman in the land should have some place to go where they don't let kids in. After all I've done for them, as well.

They're never grateful, grown-ups, no matter what you do.

Chapter Five

'Did God make Gloria Hottentot as well?'

I'VE DECIDED TO FORGIVE our Mam and Dad for being so ungrateful, as when I got up this morning, Whit Sunday, I had a new candy-striped dress, a pair of black patent leather shoes with a strap and a button to fasten them with, new white ankle socks and a new pink and white ribbon in squares.

The whole day would have been lovely if they'd have let me stop off Sunday School, but when I asked, you'd have thought I wanted to fly in an aeroplane or something. 'Of course you've got to go to Sunday School,' our Mam said. 'You're a little heathen, as it is.'

'You don't go,' I said, and our Mam said, 'Ah, I might not go now, but I had to when I was a little girl like you.' When I grow up, I won't force my children to go to Sunday School at all. If they want to go, and I bet they don't, then they can go, but if they don't, then they can stay at home with me.

'You want to learn about God, don't you?' our Lucy said, and I said, 'Why?' and she said, 'Did you hear that, Mam?' and our Mam said, 'That's what I mean, she's a little heathen. Not knowing about God's like not knowing about sweets.'

'But I can see sweets,' I said. 'I can't see God.' 'You don't have to see him,' our Mam said, and I could see she was starting to get mad. She always does when she starts talking about God. 'If I can't see him,' I said, 'then how do I know he's there ?'

'She got the slipper at school for doing that,' our Rose said. I really hate her. 'For doing what?' our Mam asked. 'For telling the teacher that if she couldn't see Rome, then how did she know it was in Italy.' 'The slipper!' our Mam said. 'Sounds to me as if she needs more than the slipper. You'd better go this afternoon as well,' she said, staring at me very hard.

'Oh Mam,' I said. 'What if I say I do believe in God then? Do I still have to go this afternoon?' But all she would say was, 'We'll see,' and I know what that means, it means I'll be going to Sunday School again this afternoon.

So I went to Sunday School this morning and I'm glad I did after all as it was very interesting. We all got there and rushed in, like we do usually. Then they sent us all out again and we had to go in one at a time, just like they do usually as well, and they said things like, 'Naow, children. Let us go in quietly. After all,' (heavy breathing) 'we mustn't forget it's the House of the Lord, must we?'

So, when we got inside and we'd sat down, they started telling us all about being sunbeams, as usual, and we sang about being sunbeams, as usual. Anyway, it was when we'd got the sunbeams out of the way at Sunday School that it started to get interesting. Little Alf Smart stands up and starts waving his hand around. 'Please, Miss,' he says, and he's hopping about from one foot to the other. 'Please, Miss,' and the brown-haired teacher with the brown hair-ribbon says, 'Now, Alfred, sit down until Mr Greybroom has finished telling you about the wondrous works of Jesus.'

Mr Greybroom, who is really the brown hair-ribbon teacher's Dad, glared down at poor little Alf and says, 'Come, come. Is it too much to expect a little peace and quiet?' and I thought, he's not going to get much peace and quiet this morning. So Alf sits down and then, in the middle of all that peace and quiet, there was this noise like running water, which of course it was, because poor little Alf had wet his pants.

Well, all I can say is that if Mr Greybroom and brown hair-ribbon are getting to go to heaven, then I hope I'm not. That Mr Greybroom went over to Alf and he shouted, 'What have you done, boy?' and poor little Alf says, 'Please sir, I tried to tell you, sir, and now I've wet me pants and what's our Mam going to say?' and he starts crying.

His big sister, Jezabel, was across in the other group, with the big girls and I could see her looking over. That's why when Mr Greybroom grabbed hold of poor little Alf's arm and started shaking him and shouting, 'You filthy boy,' I thought, oho! There's going to be trouble now, and there was. I wouldn't have missed going to Sunday School for anything.

Their Jezabel came rushing over and she yelled at Mr Greybroom, ''Ere, what you doing with our Alf?' and Mr Greybroom went white and dropped his hand and then he said, 'My good girl, return to your seat immediately,' and Jezabel said, 'I'm going to fetch my Dad up to you, I am. You've made our Alf cry, you have.' And their Alf was sobbing buckets. The brown hair-ribbon said to Jezabel, 'I think you ought to calm yourself and return to my sister's class,' and Jezabel said, 'Tek off,' and she picked up poor little Alf and carried him out of the hall.

There was a long wet trail behind him.

When they'd gone, it was so quiet you could have heard a pin drop and Mr Greybroom said, 'I think that'll be all for today, children. You may go now,' and I said, 'Oh, Mr Greybroom, we've only just come. Do we really have to go home now?' Because I wanted to be there when Alf Smart's Dad got up to the Sunday School. But Mr Greybroom saw right through me and he said, 'I might have expected it of you,' and brown hair-ribbon went all hoity-toity and said, 'After all we've done for you.' I said, 'What have you ever done for me, then?' and she said, 'We give up every Sunday to come here and teach you lot.'

So I stuck my tongue out at her and said I thought she was wasting her time and she said, 'Evidently. In your case, anyway.'

Anyway, we were all turfed out and the door was locked as if there were a fire somewhere. They didn't do it a minute before time either, because we could see Alf's Mam come roaring up the street like a steam roller. She's a big woman, Alf's Mam, and she's got a fist like a piece of ham, our Mam says.

So, we all hung around and Alf's Mam banged on the Sunday School door and she was crying. I couldn't understand that at all, so when I got home I asked our Mam about it, and our Mam said, 'Well, would you believe it. I don't know. You can't even send them to church without trouble of one kind or another,' and *she* went about looking all fed-up for the rest of the morning. There's no working out grown-ups, no matter which way you try it.

This afternoon, at the other Sunday School, they were telling us about being a peacemaker. That means when you see trouble, you should try and stop it. So I said, 'Like this morning?' and the teacher said, 'Why, what happened this morning?' and came and sat at the side of me for a bit. I don't mind him. He's not bad. At least he listens to you and doesn't go on about God all the time. So I told him about poor little Alf and Alf was sat there and he started sniffling and by the time I'd finished, he was crying again. And before I could say a thing, their Jezabel came through from the other class, *again*, and thumped me. I said to her, 'What did you do that for?' and she said, ''Cos you made him cry, that's why.' So I started hitting her, didn't I, and it was just like hitting the side of our house. She never budged.

So, this Sunday School teacher, he starts shouting, 'Girls, girls. Stop that, at once,' and I was that busy kicking Jezabel Smart, who is the most horrible girl I know, that when the teacher got in front of her, I kicked his leg by mistake. By, you should have seen him hop round that room.

He looked at me, when he'd finished hopping that is, and he said, 'You look as if butter wouldn't melt in your mouth, you do.' I said, 'Nobody hits me and gets away with it,' and he said, 'What have I just been teaching you?' and nobody answered. They were all too busy laughing, that's why, rotten kids. 'Come on,' he shouts, 'get your heads out of those hankies and tell me. What have I just been telling you about?' and somebody at the back said, 'Being a peacemaker, Sir,' and he said, 'Shout that, so's everyone can hear. Particularly the front row,' and glared at me. I said to him, 'No good looking at me like that, Sir. Weren't my fault,' and he said, 'No, it never is, is it?' and I thought, 'Blooming heck. School all week and this on Sunday.' I felt really fed up, and when I grow up I'm never going to go to Sunday School again as long as I live.

Of course, Gloria Hottentot has to get up, doesn't she? Her with her yellow hair and pink frock. She stands there and hangs her head down so that she can look up at Sir and she says, 'Oooooh, pleath Thir,' (she's short-tongued, our Mam says. I said, 'How can she be short-tongued, Mam, when she's got the biggest mouth in school,' and our Mam said it hadn't got nothing to do with that, so I don't know). Anyway, she says, 'Pleath, Thir, I'll tell ethrybothy what you were telling uth abouth, Thir,' and she smiles at him and I know for a fact that she spends about fifty hours every night smiling with her fingers stuck in her cheeks so that she'll get dimples. Anyway, she's got them and they're horrible, but as she's horrible as well, they match each other a treat.

Anyway, Sir says, 'Very well, dear' – yuk, yuk, yuk – 'you tell us,' and she stands there and tells us all practically word for word what he'd said and Jezabel's standing there looking as if she'd like to kill me and I'm standing there wondering if they'll miss me at home when I'm dead and gone, which I shall be after Jezabel's finished with me. I think I'll go down fighting like they did in the war, but it doesn't make me feel any happier and I wish I'd kept my big mouth shut. I never meant to make poor little Alf cry but their Jezabel always says, 'I don't care what you *meant*. All I know is what you *did*,' and then thumps you.

By the time that horrible Gloria Hottentot (that's not her real name – Hottentot. Somebody christened her that. I think the Hottentots live in Africa or somewhere. Anyway, I think G.H. looks like them), yes, that Gloria's finished talking and smiling and twisting round on her horrible little pink shoes – yuk, yuk, yuk – Sir pats her on the head and says, 'Well done, dear,' and everybody pretends they're going to be sick and Sir starts shouting again. I don't know about angels and that, but it seems to me we could do with some of them down here to take Sunday School. I think they'd be a lot more useful than flying around heaven playing those fiddles, or whatever they play.

Anyway, I thought, well, seeing as how I'm in church anyway, I'll ask for a miracle because it says in the Bible that if you ask then it shall be given. So I stood there and I shut my eyes. (You can't pray with your eyes wide open and I don't know why. Perhaps it's so that you can't see God if He comes down and listens to you.) I said, 'Dear God,' and then I thought, I wonder if that's right, but whichever way I tried it, I kept coming back to that, so I said, 'Dear God. Please will you strike Jezabel Smart down dead before the end of Sunday School. Thank you very much,' and I opened my eyes and stared at Jezabel and she stared back at me and then I suddenly thought, I wonder if God knows who she is? He might not be able to find her with all these people about, so I closed my eyes again and said, 'She's the one with the black hair.' Then there was this terrible noise.

I thought, 'I'll always believe in God now,' and started thanking him because I thought it was Jezabel being struck down dead. But when I opened my eyes, it wasn't. It was something ever so much better. It was little Alf. He'd wet his pants again and it had gone all over Gloria Hottentot's white socks and little pink shoes and she was going mad. She must have been because she hit little Alf and then Alf's Jezabel nearly went spare. What a carry on. Anyway, Jezabel forgot all about me, but she didn't forget about Gloria.

The teacher had to take her home and Jezabel walked right behind them all the way and she kept shouting, 'You can't hold his hand for ever,' and, 'I'll get you, don't you worry,' and all you could hear from Gloria the Gobstopper was her shoes squelching as she walked.

I could change my mind about Sunday School. It's not been a bad day at all today.

Chapter Six

'Where did our Pete find this tiger?'

I THINK IT'S JUST AS WELL I went to Sunday School yesterday because I got run over today. See what I mean about Guardian Angels though, don't you? I mean, where was mine at the time, that's what I'd like to know?

I'm lying on the sofa writing this. Our Mam says I've aged her ten years in a day. I don't know why they always get on at me. It's not my fault. I was just crossing the road and this motor-bike ran over me. So I laid there and this lad jumped off and he's shouting, 'Oh! Oh! What have I done? What have I done?' and I looked up at him and I said, 'You've blooming well run over me, that's what you've done,' and I sat up and then I opened my mouth and started yelling because there was all blood down my legs and it was dripping off my hands and when I touched my face that was bleeding as well.

Our Mam came rushing out of the house like a reindeer, and she picks me up and rushes back with me and lays me on the sofa and before you can move, the kitchen's full of everybody in the street. I bet you can't guess who were at the front of the queue though? Yes, that's right. Old Flo and Granny Bates and Mrs Elston. Mrs Elston says, 'I think I'm going to be sick,' and Old Flo says to her, 'If you're going to be sick, you go off home and be sick in your own house, my girl,' and Mrs Elston screwed up her mouth and said, 'Well, it's passed off now,' and she stayed.

Old Flo and Granny Bates were ever so nice. Old Flo got a big basin of water and she bathed all my legs and arms and all my face. It hurt like mad, but what I was really crying for was because my new Whit Sunday frock had a tear in it. Our Mam says, 'Shush, shush, my little lass,' and she starts blinking her eyes very fast and I thought, 'Oh, she's going to cry,' so I started crying, which I always do when our Mam cries because I can't help it. And then, Old Flo says to our Mam, 'There, there, now. Look, Gran's got you a nice cup of tea,' and our Mam kept saying, 'I don't want no tea. Fetch a doctor,' and Old Flo says, 'We've sent for him but there's nothing broken. She'll be all right,' and I thought, there she goes again. She'll ask me to get up and mend the fire next, but she didn't.

Anyway, when the doctor came, it was all over, bar the shouting, and our Dad was doing plenty of that because that young lad on the bike couldn't drive and he'd borrowed the bike from his mate and there were bobbies outside and everything. What a carry on.

The nice doctor came, the one with the cool hands, and he looked at me and then at our Mam and he said, 'How many children have you got?' Our Mam said, 'Six,' and he said, 'I thought it was six. Why is it always this one that gets into bother?' and our Mam smiled at him, just a little smile, and then she says, 'She's been more trouble than the other five put together and that's a fact.' I thought, 'What a thing to say,' and I felt really fed up, so I started crying again, and then our Mam hugged me and said, 'But I wouldn't part with her for a five-pound note.' So then I stopped crying and felt a lot better.

The doctor gave me some medicine and I fell asleep. I've only just woken up again. All our lads and our Lucy and Rose bought me sweets and some comics and our Dad even gave me some grapes, which I gave to Mam, but she made me eat them, which I'm glad about because they were ever so good.

Our Mam says my new frock will mend just like new again. Old Flo and Granny Bates have been sat in the kitchen all day and every time they think I can hear what they're talking about, one of them looks over at me and says, 'Now shush, my little lass,' and I have to close my eyes again and pretend to be asleep. I shall be glad when I can get up. I don't like being in bed and I've been on this sofa all day.

I was glad when our Pete got home tonight. He'd brought a rabbit home from the farm with him. It's a real big one. I thought it was still alive and I said to him, 'Can I hold it?' and he said, 'All right' and when he gave it me, it was dead. I screamed my head off and our Mam said, 'You'd think you'd have more sense at your age,' and our Pete said, 'Well, I'll bring her a kitten tomorrow. The farm cat's just had a litter.' So our Mam said, 'That's all right then.' But I thought, I don't want a kitten. It might scratch our Prince. Prince is our dog and I love him. But then, nobody ever asks me what I want because I'm only a *child*.

Our Mam looked at the rabbit and she said, 'That'll make a nice stew,' and I said to her, 'I don't want none, Mam,' and she said, 'Don't you be so foolish, my lass. You're having some whether you want it or not,' and I thought, when I grow up, I shall never eat anything I don't want in all my life.

So, that poor little rabbit had to be made into a stew and our Pete said, 'Well, it might as well go into a stew, mightn't it, 'cos it couldn't run about and play any more, could it?' And I said to him, 'Did you kill it?' and he said, 'No,' and I said, 'Well, how did it get to be dead then?' and he said, 'It died of old age, my old love,' and I said, 'Oh, well, that's different then. I'll eat some if it died of old age.'

'Yes,' he said. 'I was standing there, in the middle of this field, and I sees this rabbit coming towards me.' He looked at me to see if I was listening properly because he likes you to listen properly, our Pete, and not just keep saying, 'Yes, yes,' and not listen at all. 'Go on,' I said, 'I'm listening,' and he went on, 'And I watched it and I thought, by, there's something queer about that rabbit and then I saw what it was.'

'What was it?' I asked, and he said, 'I don't rightly know if I should tell you,' and I shouted, 'Maaaaammmmm,' and he said, 'Oh, all right then. So, I sees what's wrong with it. It's walking on a pair of crutches.' I looked at him and he looked at me and he said, 'Well, do you want me to go on?' and I said, 'I think so,' and he went on, 'Well, there it is, on these crutches, and it got right up to my feet and I heard it say, "Oh, by gum, I can't step over them hills," and it fell over backwards, with its paws in the air. So I picked it up and I says to it, "Are you all right?" and it says, "Nay lad, I'm not, and I were just on way to Post Office for me pension as well."'

So, I looked at our Pete and he looked at me and he said, 'What do you reckon to that?' and I said, 'I reckon I'm not as daft as I look,' and he laughed and said, 'Well, anyway, I'll bring you that kitten tomorrow.'

So now I m going to get a kitten I don't want and every time it widdles on the floor, everybody will shout at *me* and say, 'It's your kitten. You should clean up after it,' and I'll spend all my entire life knee-deep in disinfectant and floor cloths and newspaper just like I did with our Prince. But I love our Prince and I never minded doing it for him. I don't feel like doing it for a kitten though.

We had rabbit stew and dumplings for dinner and I kept seeing that poor old rabbit with its paws in the air talking to our Pete. Our Mam nearly went mad with our Pete. 'Why won't you eat it?' she said, and I told her about it going to collect its pension on crutches and she started laughing and then she said to our Pete, 'You'll have to buy her something from the shop,' and he said, 'I've only got enough money for the pictures, Mam,' and she said, 'You should have thought of that before you tormented her,' and he moaned and groaned until in the end I said, 'Oh, I feel like my stew now, Mam,' and she brought it out of the oven and said to our Pete, 'And you may think yourself very lucky, my lad,' and our Pete actually patted my head – yuk, yuk, yuk. Next time, I won't eat it and then he'll have to spend his picture money. They're all scraping up money to go out with tonight, and because I'm downstairs I have to lie here and watch them get ready. First our Pete and then our Tone. Our Pete put so much brilliantine on his hair I said to him, 'If ever you fell on your head, you'd slide down the street,' and he said I'd more rattle than an empty tin can. 'Empty tin cans don't rattle,' I said. 'They do when you kick them,' he said and glared at me. So I thought I'd better keep quiet for a bit.

Our Tone took about seventeen hours to get ready. Even our Mam said, 'I've never known anybody take so long getting ready to go anywhere before. If you were getting wed you couldn't take much longer.' Our Lucy said, 'Oh, haven't you heard? He's got a girlfriend as well now,' and our Tone jumped across the kitchen with the flannel in his hand and he stuffed it down our Lucy's back. She wasn't half mad. She was crying she was so mad.

Our Mam says to her, 'Now, it serves you right for tale telling,' and our Lucy said, 'I wasn't tale telling. I was only . . .'

'Tale telling!' our Tone yelled at her.

Our Lucy sniffed and said to our Mam, 'If you wouldn't mind taking that wet flannel from out of my jumper, Mother,' and she just stood there scowling at our Tone. I thought, poor old Tone. I bet something pretty horrible's going to happen to you, because she's a rum one to cross, our Lucy.

Anyway, they all went out at last and we were sat there, me and our Mam and Dad and Rose and Joe, listening to a ghost story on the wireless. Our Mam blew out the gas lamp and we were sat in the firelight and it was real still and spooky, when all of a sudden there was this terrible screaming and yelling in the passage. You could tell it was in the passage because when you make a noise in there, it echoes.

'Whatever's that?' our Mam shouted, and she was scrambling around for matches to light the gas mantle and she kept shouting to our Dad, 'Go and see who it is, John! Go on! Quickly!' and our Dad shot up out of his chair saying, 'All right, Lissy, all right. Don't panic! Don't panic!' to our Mam, because he was half asleep. He'd dropped off sitting there all quiet and waking up so sudden, he hardly knew where he was.

So, our Dad shakes his head, marches through the kitchen, picks up his big torch and flings open the back door. He shines the torch down the passage and we're all trying to see round him and there's our Tone and Lucy rolling over and over down the passage, and standing against the wall like a weed is a tall, thin girl. She's going, 'Ooooh! Ooooh!' and our Dad strides down the passage and gives me the torch to hold.

First, he hauls our Lucy to her feet and then our Tone and

he has to hold them apart because they're both still trying to get at each other. 'I'll kill you,' our Tone roars and our Lucy laughs in just the way our Tone hates. 'Ha, ha!' she goes. 'You and whose army?' Our Dad drags them both up the passage and into the back yard.

By now all the back doors are open and everybody in the street seems to be in the yard. Mrs Elston shouts to our Lucy, 'That's right, my girl, stand up for your rights,' and our Mam says to her, 'Oh yes, you encourage her to behave like a hooligan, I should,' and she marches over to our Lucy and says to her, 'In!' Our Lucy takes one look at our Mam's face and she goes all quiet and walks into the house.

Our Dad says to Tone, 'I think you'd better go in as well, lad,' and our Tone nods. Then our Dad says, 'Is that little lass with you?' and he looks at this tall, thin girl who's still standing against the wall in the passage. Tone says, 'Yes,' and our Dad says, 'Go and get her then. You'll have some explaining to do there, I shouldn't wonder.' Our Mam says, 'Not as much as he's going to have to do in that house,' and she waits till our Tone fetches this girl up the passage and then we all go into the house and our Mam shuts the back door. Bang!

We're all crowded into the room and I get back on the sofa before our Mam sees I'm walking around. I see this tall, thin girl is crying. There's all tears falling down her face. It's the first time I've seen anybody cry without making a noise.

'Now,' says our Mam. 'What happened?' Our Tone is scowling and our Lucy's face is as white as a sheet and her lips are all tight when she's not talking, but when she tries to say anything they go quiver, quiver. This other girl is standing there and she suddenly points at our Lucy and says, 'It was her!' Our Mam turns round and looks at Lucy and Lucy sort of shrugs her shoulders and screws up her face and says, 'Well,' and then it all came out.

Our Lucy had followed Tone to the pictures and sat

behind him and his girl-friend and just when they were kissing and cuddling each other, she stuffed an ice cream down the back of his shirt, but half of it went into his girl-friend's ear and they'd all been thrown out of the pictures because of the noise. They'd even stopped the film in the middle and turned on the lights because our Tone was chasing Lucy up and down the aisles.

I should have liked to have seen that and our Mam says to me, 'You stop laughing else you'll go straight to bed, poorly or no poorly.' So I shut up and got right down under the covers where they couldn't see if I was laughing or not.

Anyway, it all ended up with our Lucy being made to pay for a new shirt for our Tone out of her paper money that she gets for taking out the papers in the night and morning, which will keep her at home for the next month, our Mam said, and our Tone having to say he was sorry to that girl and our Lucy having to say she was sorry to that girl as well.

Then, our Mam said it was time for some supper and she said to the girl, 'Do you want some supper, love?' and the girl said, 'I'd rather go home, I think,' and our Tone put his fist up at Lucy and luckily for him, our Mam didn't see it.

That girl went out saying to our Mam, 'I've never been so ashamed in all my life,' and I looked at our Lucy and she looked at me and I said to her, 'I don't like her either,' and Lucy grinned and said, 'I shouldn't have done that, though,' and went to bed before our Mam came back.

But that was no good and I could have told her so because all that happened then was our Mam said, 'And where is that little madam?' and I said, 'I'm here, Mam,' because usually it's me she calls that. She smiles at me and says, 'Just for once, it's not you,' and I said, 'I don't know where she is,' and she says, 'I'll find her,' and she went straight upstairs and didn't come down again for ages.

My legs hurt that much from where that motorbike ran

over them that I couldn't get to sleep that night and every time our Lucy and Rose moved, they kicked me. So in the end I woke our Mam up and she said, 'Come on. I'll make you a bed up on the sofa,' so me and our Mam slept downstairs in the front room all night. Our Mam slept in the big old armchair and when it was half-past five, she went and shouted our Pete up. He came tumbling down the stairs as if he'd got his eyes shut.

'What's up, my old love?' he says to me when he saw me lying on the sofa and I told him my legs hurt. 'That kitten'll be very nice then, won't it?' he says and I says, 'What about our Prince?' and our Pete says, 'Well, what about him?' and I says, 'He doesn't like cats,' and our Pete starts getting mad then and saying, 'If you don't want a kitten, just say so.' So I said, 'I don't want one,' and he went, 'Oh! Oh! Never grateful, people in this house aren't,' and then he says, 'Well, you're getting one anyway, whether you want one or not,' and I thought, 'Boy, I'll be glad when I'm better and nobody wants to bring me things any more.'

Anyway, our Pete slammed out of the back door and our Mam says, 'Why don't you want a kitten?' and I says, 'I don't really like them, Mam,' and our Mam says, 'Well, you're a funny one, aren't you?' and everybody in the whole wide world seems to agree with that.

Anyway, I was lying there wondering why people can't fly, because it would be very handy when you'd hurt your legs if you could fly, when our Pete comes back for his breakfast and hanging from his hand was this old brown sack with a lump in it and the lump was going 'Spit! Spit! Psssst! Yowl! Grrrr!' and our Mam looks at the sack and she says, 'What's that?' and our Pete says, 'It's that kitten for madam there, for a pet for her,' and our Mam said, 'Are you sure?' and our Pete says, 'Why? Why?' and our Mam says, 'Oh, nothing, nothing. Only it doesn't sound very happy, does it?' Personally, I thought it sounded as if it had gone mad but nobody asked me, of course.

Our Pete walks over to me and he upturns this sack and this kitten drops out on to my knee. I thought it was a baby tiger the way it carried on. It spat and scratched and clawed me until I had to let it go. It's all striped, as well, and it looks like a tiger.

Our Mam looked at it and then she looked at my arms which were covered in scratches and she said, 'Are you sure it's all right?' and our Pete said, 'Of course it's all right. It's *her*.' (pointing at me), 'She doesn't know how to handle them.' 'Oooooh!! Make way for Jungle Boy,' I said.

By now the kitten was swinging along the top of the curtains and our Mam says to Pete, 'Get it down from there, it's tearing all my curtains,' and our Pete reached up for it and it went, 'Pssst!' and he jumped back as if he'd been shot. I laughed like a drain but I soon stopped when our Mam said, 'As you think it's so funny, you get it down,' and I tried and the rotten thing bit me.

I screamed blue murder and our Dad came in from work and said, 'Why is she always screaming when I come home?' and our Mam had just started saying, 'Whatever do you mean, always screaming?' when the kitten swung across the curtains and made a jump for the mantelpiece and our Dad looked at it and said, 'I don't believe it,' and our Mam said, 'It's true. It won't come down and it's bitten madam there and scratched our Pete.' So our Dad said, 'Leave it to me,' and he went to get it and trod accidentally on our Prince who'd just poked his nose out from under the table to see if he'd imagined hearing a cat in the house. Our Dad went flying and our Prince went scuttering round the table howling his poor little head off.

'You big bully,' I shouted at our Dad and our Mam reached over and slapped my arm. 'Well, he is,' I yelled and I had to pick our poor old Prince up and love him better. Our Dad sat on the sofa and he kept saying, 'If ever a man suffered,' and our Mam snapped at our Pete to get that cat out of the house, but we couldn't catch it.

We got it down in the end because our brilliant Pete threw an old towel over it and it was hissing and scratching inside it and our Mam looked at Pete and said, 'And you brought that home as a pet?' Our Pete said, 'It was *her* that done it,' and I said, 'Oh yes, blame me, it's always me' (which they always say it is).

Anyway, our Dad said, 'You'd better take it back to the farm,' so our Pete took it back after he'd had his breakfast and the farmer said to our Dad when he saw him later that he'd told our Pete his farm cats were really spiteful and he didn't think it would do as a pet, but our Pete wouldn't be told.

'And that's the trouble,' our Dad said when he'd finished telling our Mam the story. 'They never will be told, any of them. We were never like that when we were kids,' and I thought, Oh heck, here we go again, and our Dad goes on and on about how they were all so wonderful when they were little kids.

They sound really horrible to me and I don't know how they ever got to make any friends, they were so good. Although I don't have many friends at all – any friends I suppose – and our Rose always says, 'That's because you're so bad, it's more trouble than it's worth to be friends with you.' So I don't know.

Chapter Seven

'Could I really have blown up all the seaside, Mam?'

Our Mam said, 'It's a good job your legs are strong enough for you to walk on now, isn't it?' and I said, 'Why?' and she said, 'Have you forgotten? We go on the seaside trip on Sunday,' and I had forgotten and it's the nicest thing that's happened in ages.

We go every year and it's smashing. Everybody's going. All our family and everybody in the street. Our Mam said, 'Don't you eat too many shrimps this time,' and I said I wouldn't because I ate too many last year and I wished I was dead all the way home. Granny Bates sits next to me in the bus because she's always wanting things out of her bag and she says, 'Your legs are younger than mine,' but they don't feel it when we get out. I have to get up and down, up and down, about five million times for her.

First, she wants a drink of tea. I said to her, 'What would you do if you were in the desert, Granny?' and she said, 'However would I get to be in the desert?' and I said, 'Well, you won't, will you, but what would you do if you did?'

'Did what?' she said.

'Find yourself in the desert,' I said. 'What would you do without your tea?' and she said, 'Oh, you can always get a cup of tea, no matter where you are,' so I asked our Mam later if Granny had ever gone to school and she said, 'Why?' and I said, 'Because she says you can always get a nice cup of tea, even in the desert, and you can't,' I said. 'It's all sand.'

'Perhaps she didn't go to school,' our Mam says. 'But she's never had to wittle about whether or not she'd get a cup of tea in the desert before, so I shouldn't bother her about it now.'

But Granny Bates brought it up again herself and says, 'Here, Lissy, what would I do if I were in the desert and wanted a cup of tea?' and our Mam glared at me and said, 'You little devil. I told you to leave well enough alone,' and then she said to Granny Bates, 'Now, Granny. When are you ever going to be in the desert?' and Granny said, 'You're right there,' and then she said to me, 'I don't think I'll buy you an ice-cream today.' So I said, 'Why not ?' and she said because I was nothing but a trial and a worry.

Anyway, it's going to be different this year. I asked our Mam if I could sit next to her and she said, 'Oh no. Your Dad always sits next to me,' and I said, 'Well, can I sit with you halfway and our Dad the other half,' and she said, 'No, because Granny Bates'll have your Dad up and down, up and down, and he won't have a minute's peace.' So I said, 'But I don't get a minute's peace either,' and she said, 'Your legs are younger than your Dad's.'

'But I got run over by a motor-bike,' I said and tried to look poorly and sad. She frowned at me for a minute and then she said, 'So you did,' and she told our Dad he'd have to sit with Granny halfway and I'd sit the other half because of my poorly legs and our Dad looked at me and said, 'That's not the only thing that's going to be poorly about that young madam if she keeps this up,' and our Mam said, 'Now, John,' and he frowned at me and I started crying and then he had to put me on his knee and say he was sorry and I was to stop crying else he'd get in bother with our Mam so I stopped.

I didn't want to push my luck too far.

I thought Sunday would never come but it did. First thing I thought when I woke up was, no Sunday School today, and then I thought, Cleethorpes! I jumped out of bed and rushed downstairs and when I went into the kitchen they were all there drinking tea and eating toast and dripping and I says to our Mam, 'Weren't you going to take me then?' and she says, 'Of course we were. I was just letting you have another five minutes,' but our horrible Rose said, 'There's no breakfast left for you. We've eaten it all. We were going to sneak out and leave you behind in bed, fast asleep.'

Then they all started laughing and our Mam said, 'Stop tormenting the child,' and I said to our Rose, 'I'd rather stop at home than go anywhere with you, Spotty,' and our Rose said, 'Mam! Mam! She's name calling again,' and our Mam says, 'For goodness sake, stop it, both of you.' Then she said to me, 'And you'll go back to bed, madam, if you don't behave yourself.' I thought, what a life when you've got brothers and sisters, but I thought I'd better not say any more so I pulled a face at our Rose instead and she hit me on the head with a teaspoon.

I said to her, 'I bet you think I'm an egg, don't you?' and she said, 'If you were, I'd cut your head off with a knife and not just bash it with a spoon,' and our Mam went, 'Rose!'

and our Rose had to say she was sorry and I stood there trying to look all hard done by and our Mam said to our Rose, 'Don't you ever let me hear you say anything like that again,' and our Rose said no, Mam, she wouldn't.

Our Mam says to me, 'One more word out of you, young lady, one more word!' and I thought, 'Oh boy, this is going to be a long day.'

Our Mam always gets worried that we'll all miss the bus so we had to stand outside Mr Banks's shop at a quarter to six and we weren't going till six o'clock and you can practically touch Mr Banks's shop from our front-room window anyway, and everybody was saying, 'Oh, Mam. Why do we have to stand there gawping at everybody? We can see when the bus comes from here,' and our Mam said, 'I know you can see when the bus comes, but folks aren't going to queue up behind us here, are they, and you know what you lot are like for sitting near the window.'

So, we all trooped out and stood there waiting for the bus and we weren't the first at that either. There were all the Byelows for a start and there's hundreds of them. 'Not much chance of getting a window seat here,' our Lucy muttered and she and our Rose started saying they weren't going if they couldn't sit together. I said, 'I should have thought you saw enough of each other at home without sitting together as well,' and Pam Byelow shouted to our Rose, 'Who you sitting with, Rosie?' and our Rose wouldn't answer her because she'd called her Rosie. Our Mam was standing there trying to pretend she hadn't heard Pam Byelow talk to our Rose but in the end she had to say something. I thought she was going to burst until she did.

'That young Pam's talking to you,' she said to our Rose. 'I know she is,' our Rose said, 'but my name is Rose, not Rosie.'

'It wouldn't hurt to answer her though, would it?' our Mam said, and Rose said, 'I'm not speaking to anybody who calls me Rosie,' and so our Mam said she didn't know what things were coming to and if she'd ever been so bad mannered, *her* mother would soon have nipped it in the bud, and our Rose glared at poor old Pam Byelow until she stopped shouting at her.

'I don't know why she wants to sit with you,' I said, 'because I'd sooner sit with a monkey than sit with you,' and our Mam just got the back of my legs right. I didn't know she was behind me and she said, 'That took you by surprise, young lady,' and our Rose laughed her stupid head off and our Mam said it was all her fault anyway for being so rude to poor old Pam Byelow and that she'd better watch her step for the rest of the day because she was never too big, and, no, she never would be, and our Dad said, 'Oh, Lissy, Lissy. You'll wear yourself out checking them kids,' and our Mam said, 'They're going to grow up decent if it kills me,' and then she looked at us all thoughtful and said, 'and them as well.'

So I had to sit with Granny Bates and even though I *told* our Dad when we were halfway there, he wouldn't come and change seats. When our Mam said, 'Now, John, I think you'd better,' he said he wouldn't, not for any money and that the exercise would be good for my legs. I must have got Granny Bates's bag down a million times between our house and Cleethorpes. The bus stopped at a cafe and we all got out and had some tea and all us kids had some pop and it was so good that I had three bottles.

We were going really fast and everybody was saying, 'We shall be there before we know where we are,' when I thought, 'I wish I hadn't had all that pop', and, of course, when I asked our Mam when the bus was going to stop again, she said, 'We've only just stopped. He won't stop again till we get to Cleethorpes,' and I said to her, 'He'll have to stop, Mam, because I want to go to the lavatory.' She nearly had a fit.

She started going red and then she said to our Dad, 'If I

don't leave that young madam behind this afternoon, it won't be for the want of trying,' and I thought, ho, yes, very nice I'm sure.

Anyway, our Dad went down to the driver and the driver started shouting and when I was getting out, he said to our Mam, 'I hope she's not going to do this tonight. I've got a home to go to as well, you know,' and our Mam said, 'What's a few minutes to you?' and we had to go behind this hedge. It wasn't very nice and I kept thinking someone would come along and see me and our Mam just stood there saying, 'If I've told you once about drinking pop when you're on a bus, I've told you a thousand times,' and I kept saying, 'Yes, Mam,' and a rotten old stinging nettle stung my legs, and by the time we got back on the bus our Mam wasn't saying a single word and neither was I because I was fed up to the back teeth.

Anyway, just after that, another little kid had to go to the lavatory as well so they had to stop the bus again and the driver kept shouting and raving about how we were going to be all day getting there and was anybody worried about seeing the sea after all, and perhaps we'd all be happier if he parked the bus in a field, and everybody started telling him to shut up, little kids couldn't help it, so when he had to stop the bus for Granny Bates, he nearly had a fit.

'I wish he would,' our Mam said, when she and Granny Bates got back into the bus. 'Miserable old devil!' But he didn't, although he stayed bright red all the way there.

Anyway, we got there in the end and I asked our Mam if I could walk on the sands on my own and she said, all right, but I wasn't to go too far away. So I started walking. I just wanted to be on my own for a bit.

I hadn't gone very far when I saw this funny thing lying on the sand. It was big and round and it had all pointed spikes sticking out all over it and it was made of iron because I bashed it with a stone and it went, *clunk, clunk.* It had a funny cap on it as well and I tried to get it off but it wouldn't budge. I thought, rotten old thing. Neither use nor ornament, so I started using it as a target and pretended I was a dive-bomber and every time I was near it, I dropped a bomb on it. The bombs were only stones off the beach but they made a good loud noise, and I had a good time and when I'd finished playing, it came in useful for leaning against.

So I was just sitting on top of it when our Dad comes walking down the beach and he starts shouting, 'Get off that. Get off it,' and I waved to him and pretended not to hear. I never *asked* him to come looking for me. You'd never believe all the fuss that went on next.

Our Mam came rushing down the beach and she was shouting to our Dad and screaming at me and I thought, 'What have I done now?' and so I burst into tears because I hate anybody shouting at me and then our Mam and Dad came up and our Dad picked me up and carried me away and there was the police there and some soldiers and everything, and the next thing, everybody on the entire whole beach had to get off it and our Lucy said, 'Trust you to clear the beach. There can't be anybody else in the world who could do that,' and I thought, well, I don't know what I've done.

And then our Tone says, 'Do you know what that was, what you were playing with?' and I said, 'No, but it weren't much good, whatever it was,' and he said, 'It would have been if it had blown up,' and I looked at him and said, 'Why should it have blown up?' and he said, 'Because it was a mine, that's why,' and I said, 'I don't feel very well.'

Our Joe said, 'You ought to have let her get blown up now, Mam. Save us all a lot of trouble later,' and our Mam said, 'Well, I don't know how I'm going to keep her in one piece and that is a fact,' and I thought, well, it's not my fault, and then nobody spoke to me for ages because they couldn't go on the beach on account of me.

I said to them, 'You want to blame the Germans. They were the ones who put it there,' and our Mam said, 'It had to be you to find it though, didn't it?' and our Tone said, 'If she'd been in the war, it wouldn't have lasted five and twenty minutes. Everybody would have surrendered. Ha, ha, ha!'

I could have been an angel by now flying round heaven playing a fiddle and nobody would be bothered. Our Lucy said, 'An angel! They'll not let you into heaven. Not if they know what's good for them, that is,' and our Pete said, 'I can just see it now. Her getting up there and St Peter saying, 'Yes?' and her saying, 'It's me,' and St Peter opening the gate and saying, 'You've come to the wrong place, you have. Down below.' Then they all started laughing again and our Mam said, 'Stop tormenting her,' but I *don't care*. I'm going to be rich and famous when I grow up and I shan't even speak to them when I pass them on the street, so there.

Anyway, because we couldn't go on the beach for ages, we walked round the town and I managed to lose them all in one of the shops. So I went and had a great big ice-cream cornet and a stick of rock, peppermint rock it was, and it was pink and white, just like usual, you know, and then I bought a hat and it had *Kiss me Quick* on the front of it but nobody did. I thought, what a rotten waste of money, but I left it on because you never know.

Then I had to find our Mam and everybody because it was tea-time and I was starving hungry and anyway I hadn't got any money left even though we'd all been given five shillings each when we got on the bus.

Our Tone said, 'Come on the big dipper with me,' and I said, 'I haven't any money left,' and he said, 'I'll treat you,' and I went on with him and when I got off I wished I was dead. But I wished I was dead a long time before I got off. I cut my head open on the back of the seat I was in and our Tone looked at me and he said, 'I'm never taking you on anything else,' and when I got off, I said to our Mam 'Look at my head, Mam, it's bleeding,' and she went all white and said, 'I give up,' and we had to go to the St John's man and he fixed it up all right.

I've decided I don't like the seaside.

We didn't get back home until nearly midnight and I was so tired I couldn't open my eyes. Anyway, I was sick three times coming back on the bus and so was Granny Bates. She kept groaning, 'Oh, I knew I didn't ought to have had those fish and chips. Oh dear, oh dear, oh dear!' I went and sat with our Dad and the bus had to stop about a million times because all the kids and Granny Bates had eaten too much.

Then – yuk, yuk, yuk – that stupid twerp Danny Howard from Shore Street grabbed me and tried to kiss me and I said, 'What do you think you're doing?' and I bashed him right in the face and he hit me back and said, 'I was trying to give you a kiss,' and I said, 'Blooming cheek!' He pulled my *Kiss me Quick* hat off and said, 'What's that say, then?' and I said, 'That doesn't mean you. That only means handsome people. Not horrible ugly mugs like you,' and he hit me again and I said, 'I hope the bus runs over you and squashes you flat,' and then I had to run back to our Mam because he looked as if he were going to murder me.

Huh! Cheeky devil! Still, it was a day out. I suppose it was all right. Anyway, thank goodness, that's it till next year.

Chapter Eight

'Why did that burglar shout for the bobbies?'

Things have been very quiet since we came back from the seaside but I'm glad to say they looked up a bit yesterday.

The man next door jumped out of his bedroom window last night. He stood on the ledge and shouted, 'I've had enough I tell you. I'm going to put an end to it all,' and Mrs Elston, who he's married to, shouted, 'Don't jump, Fred! Don't jump,' and the old chap who belongs to the Sally Army (that's the Salvation Army), he comes rushing out of the house pulling up his trousers and shouting to his wife, 'Get me braces, Ethel! Get me braces.' Then he sort of skidded to a halt underneath the bedroom window and shouts to Mr Elston, 'Now then, Fred. Don't be foolish,' and then Fred (Mr Elston, that is) shouts, 'I'm done for,' and jumped.

I don't know what all the fuss was about because when we were trying out our Mam's sheets to see if they made good parachutes, we jumped off the bedroom window-sill as well. Mind you, it hurt a bit because the sheets didn't behave like parachutes at all. Where we got hurt most though was where our Mam clobbered us for using her sheets in the first place. They're not very high, our houses, you see. There are only two rooms downstairs and two rooms up and if you're a little bit taller than usual and you've got a stool, you can touch the bottom of the bedroom window-sill with your hand.

Anyway, Mr Elston (Fred, that is) jumped off the bedroom window-sill and you'd never believe the commotion. His wife, Mrs Elston, ran round and round in circles and she was shouting and yelling, 'Oh dear, oh dear! Whatever's going to become of us all now?' And then she suddenly stopped and threw her hand up to her head and said, 'Dear heavens! The insurance! I never paid him last week,' and leaving Mr Elston (Fred, that is) on the floor, she rushed in to find her insurance book.

Our Mam picked Mr Fred Elston up off the floor and brushed him down. 'I had to do it,' he was saying. 'I had to do it,' and then his wife, who he's married to, Mrs Fred Elston, she came rushing back into the street, waving the insurance book in the air. 'Don't you ever do that again,' she said to Mr Fred Elston. 'I wouldn't have got a penny off the insurance if anything had happened to you.' When our Mam and Dad came in, I noticed they were laughing their heads off. You can't make people out sometimes, can you?

Of course people don't jump out of their bedroom windows every day but it makes a change when they do.

Our Mam says it's not been Mrs Elston's week at all this week because Mrs Elston's husband, Fred, who jumped out of the window, only went back to work this morning and Mrs Elston found a burglar in her kitchen when she got back from up town shopping.

I says to our Mam, 'All the exciting things happen to other

people,' and she said, 'We can do without those kind of exciting things, I am sure,' and she looked at me and said, 'He might have stolen you,' and I said, 'I didn't know burglars stole little girls,' and our Mam laughed and said, 'They don't, you daft thing. Anyway,' she said, 'what would you have done if he had?' and I said, 'I'd have shouted our Prince,' and then me and our Mam looked at our Prince who was having a nice little snooze in front of the fire and our Mam said, 'Yes well . . .' I said, 'I don't think it would have done much good though, Mam,' and our Mam said she didn't think it would have done much good either and then she asked me where he'd got the blue bootees from that he was wearing.

So I told her about the little kids from next door coming round and asking if they could have Prince to play with. He's a black spaniel, our Prince, and he's the kindest person in the whole world. I said, 'What are you playing at?' and little Betty (the girl from next door, that is) she said, 'Mams and Dads,' and I said, 'What do you want Prince for then?' and she said, 'He's going to be the baby,' so I thought, well, poor little kids, why not, and so I shouted our Prince and he came from under the table wagging his old tail and little Betty picked him up and sat down with him on her knee, because she found she couldn't carry him. All his back legs were scraping along the floor.

They put a little hat on him with a blue pom-pom on it and a little coat and a lovely pink frock. I don't know where they got it from. Then, they put him in their dolls' pram and wheeled him up and down the street and our Prince just laid there like a great soft kid. He got fed up in the end, though, and the last I saw of them all was Betty and her little mates chasing after our Prince. He looked a right sight he did, with that bonnet and frock on. They'd even put four little bootees on his feet and now here he was, turned up in the kitchen again without any of the baby clothes except two little blue bootees. I says to our Mam, 'He's not really what you'd call a watchdog, is he, Mam?' and she said seeing as how he shoved everybody out of the way in his hurry to get under the table whenever it thundered, she thought he wasn't a watchdog at all.

Our Dad came in then and our Mam started telling him about the burglar at Mrs Elston's. 'Terrible it was, John,' she said, and then Mrs Elston came rushing round because she'd seen our Dad come home and she wanted to tell him all about her burglar herself. She said, 'I've never been so surprised in all my born days,' and our Mam said, 'It's a good job you gave him a bash on the head, Matty,' and Matty (that's a queer name, isn't it?) said, 'Well, there he were, large as life and twice as ugly, rooting through all my drawers, he were. I never felt so mad in all my life, I never.'

Anyway, this burglar was shouting for the bobbies when our Mam went round. She said, 'There was this awful noise and then I heard somebody shouting 'Help! Help!' and I went rushing round, with Granny Bates and Old Flo, who just happened to be here having a nice cup of tea, and there's Mrs Elston and she's got this fella on the floor and she's hitting him over the head with her umbrella, and it's a big heavy umbrella that one, you know, and she's got this poker in her other hand and she's shouting, "I'll show you, you devil," and it's this burglar who's shouting "Help! Help! Fetch the bobbies",' and our Mam burst out laughing and had to sit down.

It was very exciting though because they fetched the bobbies and they took this burglar away and I'm glad about that because it's a bit scary to think of burglars in the back kitchen, even if they don't steal little girls.

Our Mam and Mrs Elston and Old Flo and Granny Bates had to have some warm water and sugar with a drop of

Indian Brandee in it afterwards because our Mam said, 'All of a sudden, we were all shaking when the bobbies had been and took him away,' and they all had to go and sit down and suddenly Mrs Elston (Matty, that is) burst into tears and they were all saying, 'There, there.'

Our Dad says to our Mam and Mrs Elston, 'You sound as if you did all right between you,' and Mrs Elston said, 'I wouldn't like it to happen again though,' and our Mam said, 'I shouldn't think any more burglars will come up here. The last I heard of him, he was shouting, "It was all for nothing, anyway. She hadn't got anything worth pinching," and Mrs Elston said, "That's very true".'

We were all sitting on the step tonight when a big policeman came round the corner of the street. The one with the stripes on his arm, and he was carrying a bunch of flowers wrapped in white paper. He marched up to Mrs Elston, and we're all sat looking at him with eyes as big as buckets, our Mam said, when he says to Mrs Elston that she'd been ever so brave and he'd brought this bunch of flowers from the Cop Shop for her.

Our Mam says I must never say 'Cop Shop' again in all my life. 'Shows a lack of respect, that does,' she says. It sounds nice though, doesn't it? Cop Shop. Oh well, I suppose I'd better call it Police Station.

I was laid thinking about Mrs Elston's burglar and the policeman all last night and I thought I'd play at detectives today for a change. But now I wish I never had. I was only playing at being Sherlock Holmes and I put our Prince on a piece of string and took that old pipe out of the sideboard drawer and walked up and down the street. Well, of course, everybody laughed and that, like they always do round here, but they left me alone.

I got pretty fed up with being a detective after a bit and our Prince sat down and wouldn't get up again and I dropped the pipe and it broke, so I thought, I'll be a detective in plain clothes. So then I went and stood outside the betting shop round the corner although I know it isn't a real betting shop but a house really and I've heard our Mam say a thousand times, 'They'll end up getting caught one of these days, they will,' and I stood outside there and stared at everybody going in and out.

It was all right at first and then this old woman marches over to me and she says, 'What you staring at?' and I says, 'You!' and she went, 'Oh!' – screech, screech – and this other old woman comes up to me and says, 'What you doing?' and I muttered, 'Police.' Just like that.

This woman stares at me and she says, 'What?' and I says, 'Police,' and she says, 'Where?' and I says, 'Plain clothes,' and nods my head and winks with my left eye, although I can't really wink at all as both my eyes shut at the same time, and she suddenly goes, 'Oh, oh!' – screech, screech – as well, and she rushes into this house and starts yelling, 'Cops! Cops!' at the top of her voice and I thought the end of the world had come. All these people inside the house tried to get out of the door at the same time and they kept getting stuck and all you could see were arms and legs and bits of heads and everything, all waving about but anyway they all got out in the end.

The street went as quiet as anything. You could have heard a pin drop and then round the corner comes a police car and it's got all bobbies in it and they jump out and rush into the house.

Well, they all came out after about five minutes and the nice one, the one with the stripes on his arm, he was playing war with the other bobbies and he was saying, 'Well, somebody tipped them off. That's obvious,' and he was moaning and groaning at them and they were saying, 'Yes, Sarge. No, Sarge,' and they all looked fed up to the back teeth.

Then the nice one sees me and he says, 'And what are you

doing, young lady?' and I says, 'Nothing, please sir,' and he says, 'You haven't seen anything, have you?' and I say, 'No.' Then our Dad rushes round the corner and he grabs me and says, 'Time for bed,' and I say to him, 'What do you mean, Dad? It's only one o'clock,' and he says, 'Home!' And so I went.

Our house was packed to bursting when I got in and I got another telling off, and if that isn't rotten then I don't know what is. All because I was playing at detectives.

Still, later on, the man who lives in the house round the corner where everybody takes their bets, he knocks on our back door and our Mam says, 'What does he want? I'm not having him in the house,' and our Dad says, 'Now, now,' and goes to the door. Then this man tells our Dad that I saved him from a police raid or something and he wanted to give me a pound note and our Mam nearly had a fit. 'We don't take money in this house,' she says, all shirty and horrible, and this man says, 'Well, Missis, I just wanted to give it to her to show how grateful I am.' Our Mam says, 'You'd do better shutting down,' and he says, 'Why? If the nobs can do it, why can't we?' and our Mam wouldn't say another word.

So, I don't know what happened to that pound note. I wanted to take it and I think the man took it back with him, but I'm sure I saw him wink at our Dad and our Dad walked down to the end of the passage with him and he was grinning all over his face when he came in. He stopped grinning when he saw our Mam but all the same, he patted me on the head – yuk, yuk, yuk.

I said to our Mam, 'I don't think I'll be a detective when I grow up after all,' and she said, 'Have you told them yet?' and I said, 'Who?' and she said, 'The Police,' and I said, 'No,' and she said, 'I should. It'll take a load off their minds,' and then she started laughing. Sometimes, I find it hard to work out what families are for.

Chapter Nine

'Who loves people like Gorilla Face?'

I FELL OFF A CLIFF YESTERDAY. So, here I am back on the sofa again in the back kitchen. Our Mam says, 'I might as well tie that sofa to you, you're on it that much.' I don't seem to go to school very much and everybody says I do things on purpose so I can stay away, but I don't. Mind you, seeing as how they happen anyway, I'm glad I don't have to go to school. Life wouldn't be worth living if you got sick and had to go to school *as well*. That's enough to make you sick on its own.

We were down at the sand quarry yesterday and there are these big cliffs everybody climbs on. There was this lad there called Micky and he had this sheet in his hands and I thought, 'He's never going to jump off the cliff,' and he starts shouting, 'I'm going to jump off this cliff,' and nobody took a bit of notice because nobody thought the daft thing would. Anyway, next thing we heard was this yell, 'G-e-r-o-n-i-m-o!,' and he jumped. Went down like a bomb and never stopped. 'Course they had to take him to hospital because he broke a leg and an arm.

'Why did you do it?' his Mam was saying when she got there.

'I saw it on the pictures, Mam,' he said and then he shut his eyes and he didn't talk any more.

His Mam was sat there crying and she had to go to hospital with him. They both had to stay in as well and our Mam said to me, 'Let that be a lesson to you,' although I don't know why it should. All I was doing was looking over the edge and I slipped and slid down the cliff and then, near the bottom, I bounced off one of those bits that stick out. It was right near the bottom, though, so I didn't get hurt.

By the time our Joe got to me, I was standing up and brushing myself down and the first thing *he* does is rattle me. 'Oh, feel free,' I said. 'I fall down a cliff and get up and what do you do? Nearly knock my head off, that's all.' He starts shouting I'm a stupid great girl and I had to go home *now*, and *just wait till you get in*, and everything. So I marched home and I'm never going to speak to our Joe again as long as I live because he runs in and shouts at our Mam, 'I'm never going to look after that stupid thing again.' Our Mam says, 'Here, here. What's all this about?' She looked at me and said, 'What have you been doing?' and I said, 'Nothing, Mam, honest,' and then our Joe went and told her I'd thrown myself off the cliff.

'I never,' I said. 'I slipped,' and our Joe says, 'If I have to look after you again, I'll shove you off,' and I said, 'Oh, don't worry, you needn't look after me. I can look after myself.' Our Mam says, 'It looks like it, doesn't it?' and then I had to get on the sofa with a cup of hot sweet tea in case I was suffering from shock and wasn't showing it, and here I am. Our Joe kept shouting and shouting and saying, 'Her suffering from shock. What about me? I'm the one who should be on that sofa. She's just one big shock,' and our Mam told him to get some bread and jam and he did and every time he passed the sofa, he kicked it.

'I hate you,' he kept saying. 'Just you wait till you're better, that's all,' and I said to him, 'If you hit me, I'll tell our Mam,' and he said, 'You won't then, because you won't be able to because I'm going to knock all your teeth out.' Then I started crying and our Mam came in and said to him, 'What have you done to her?' and he said, 'Nothing, Mam, honest,' and our Mam said she didn't know why people had kids because they were nothing but a trial and a tribulation. If they're anything like our Joe, I think they are too and I don't think people should have kids like our Joe at all . . . or our Tone and Pete and Lucy and Rose, come to think of it.

'That Lucy will go too far one day,' our Mam said yesterday. She was going to the pictures and she thinks nobody knows she puts powder and lipstick on. Our Mam kept coming into the kitchen and saying, 'What's that smell? You' re not wearing powder, are you, our Lucy? and Lucy kept saying, ''Course I'm not. Anyway, I can't smell anything. Can you?' and I kept shaking my head and saying, 'No, I can't smell anything either,' mainly because our Lucy had said she' d give me twopence if I kept my big mouth shut.

Anyway, there she is, putting this powder on, and she looks at me and says, 'Make sure you don't tell our Mam,' and gives me twopence and I say, ''Course I won't.' Then she looks in the mirror and says, 'I wonder if I dare try a bit of lipstick,' and I'm sat there watching her and she says, 'I think I will,' and she puts this lipstick on, *in the house*. 'Well, I'll be working soon,' she says when I tell her our Mam'll have a fit if she catches her, but she hopped out of the back door prettty sharpish when our Mam came into the kitchen again.

But our Mam rushed after her and shouts, 'Lucy. Come back a minute. I want you to call in to Granny Bates for me,' and our Lucy came back and she had this great scarlet mouth. You never saw anything like it and our Mam put her hand over her eyes and said, 'Give me strength,' and she got hold of our Lucy by the neck and marched her back to the sink in the kitchen and she scrubbed her face with the flannel and some red hot water out of the kettle.

Our Lucy says to me, 'Wait till I get you,' and I said, 'I never said anything to our Mam.' I don't know what she'll do next, because after our Mam had scrubbed her face clean, she said, 'I shall only put it on again when I'm outside,' and our Mam says to her, 'You do, young lady, and see what happens.' But she let our Lucy go and started looking in her own handbag for a light pink lipstick, which I know our Lucy won't wear, not if it gets up and bites her, she won't.

After our Lucy had gone out, me and our Mam were sat finding pictures in the fire for a bit and then our Mam looked at me and said, 'You look all right now. Come on, let's go over and have a look at Mrs Beamer's new baby. That'll be a nice little airing for you.' So I said, 'Oh, Mam, do I have to?' and she said, 'It's a brand new baby. All little girls like new babies,' but I thought, here's one little girl who doesn't, but I didn't like to say anything because our Mam thinks anything little is lovely.

Personally, I think babies are all right when they're about four years old and you can talk to them. Till then, ugh!

Mrs Beamer's baby was just the same as all the rest. I reckon if you've seen one baby, you've seen them all.

It was a very queer looking thing and it had no hair and a bright red face and it yelled all the time I was there. I said to our Mam, 'Do they always do that?' but she was holding it and saying, 'Coochie coo,' and daft things like that to it. If I were a baby and anybody leant over me and said, 'Coochie coo,' I don't think I'd bother stopping.

I asked Mrs Beamer if I could hold it and she said, 'You will be careful, love, won't you?' and I said, 'Oh yes, Mrs Beamer,' and I had to sit on this big chair and hold it in my arms very tightly. It went redder than ever and our Mam says, 'Not too tight, you daft thing. Let the poor little mite breathe,' and I had to sit there as if I were made out of stone because every time I moved either our Mam or Mrs Beamer started telling me to be careful and mind its head.

I was glad to give it back. I can't see as they're a lot of use and they're always wet through. There was a big wet patch on my frock where I laid that baby. Our Mam said, 'You'll be able to take it walks when it's a bit older,' and I thought, who wants to take it walks. But I didn't say anything, because you're suppposed to love babies. I can't see what all the fuss is about. Boys aren't supposed to love babies so I don't know why girls should.

After I'd sat there like a statue for a bit, our Mam said I could go and play and so I thought I'd walk down to the sand quarry to see if there was anybody there and halfway down the road, who should come up but a gang from one of the other streets. Anyway, this girl, with long black plaits, she walks up to me and hits me straight in the face, so I hit her back and then all these kids start whooping and yelling and they tie me to a lamp post and say they're Indians, stupid things, and then they say they're going to burn me at the stake and they start putting all grass and paper and bits of wood round the bottom of the lamp post. Then one of them gets this match out and lights it. All that paper and everything starts burning away and I think, I don't know about getting burnt to death, I think I'll choke to death first, because the grass doesn't burn and there's clouds of smoke. Anyway, there I was spluttering and yelling and a woman from across the road leans out of her bedroom window and goes 'Oh, oh!' – screech, screech – and the next second her head vanishes and her front door flies open and these kids run in all directions, and she unties me and stamps out the fire, and she's bawling and shouting at these kids and I think, I don't feel very well.

Anyway, I'm black from top to bottom with the smoke and this woman takes me home and I'm crying like mad and when our Mam sees me, she makes this woman a cup of tea and says, 'I don't know how to thank you,' and then she starts crying and saying, 'Whatever will they do next?' Then our Joe rushes in and says, 'Where is she?' Our Mam says, 'You're supposed to be looking after her,' and he says, 'I've only just heard about it and I came looking for her straight away.' Then he says to me, 'Come on you. You're coming with me. We're going to find them kids.' I say, 'I hope you bash them, our Joe, because I've never been burnt at the stake before,' and then I have to cry again because I can still smell all that smoke and it was very, very scary.

So, we roamed all round the streets, our Joe with his pals and me. We saw them in the end and I says to our Joe, 'She's the one. That big girl with the plaits,' and our Joe grabs her and ties her to a lamp post and he says to me, 'Come on, then, you give her a good hiding,' and so I bash her as well and I think, 'I hope she doesn't live round here because when she's untied, she's going to come after me,' but I don't let that stop me bashing her there and then. I think perhaps it might be the last chance I get.

Anyway, this big girl starts yelling blue murder and an enormous woman suddenly comes out of a yard and the big girl starts yelling, 'Ooh, Mam! Oooh,' and the big woman stops that quick, I thought she'd fall over. But she didn't, and our Joe shouts to everybody, 'Run, run.' So we did, as fast as we could.

I've a feeling I haven't seen the last of that girl because I heard her shouting, 'I'll get you, Skinny Lizzie. You just wait and see if I don't.' So all I can do now is wait and see, like she says.

Our Mam says, 'She'd better not lay another finger on you,' but seeing as how she's already tried to burn me at the stake, I don't think anything our Mam says will make much difference to her. Our Dad went round to try and see if he could find her and her family later on, but he couldn't find out where they lived. I think they must be new round here because I haven't seen her before but I bet anything you like I'll be seeing her again before I'm very much older.

I think I might be a fortune teller when I grow up because when I walked into the playground this morning, there's this great big fat girl with the long black plaits staring at me as if Christmas comes three times a year and today's one of those times.

'Well, well,' she says. 'Look who's here.' Then she comes over to me and my heart's doing about a million thuds a second and I think my legs are going to give way because, honest, she's as big as our house and when she gets right up to me she says, 'I'm going to make mincemeat out of you and they'll have to take you home on a shovel,' and I look at her and say, 'And I bet you think I'm going to stand here and let you, don't you?' and she says, 'Yes, because there's nothing you can do about it, Skinny.' And she pushes me and it's just like being run over by a bus and I pick myself up and I shout, 'You want to get back to the jungle, Gorilla Face,' and she goes bright purple and says, 'Ug! Ug! Ug! I'll murder you. I'll flatten you. I'll kill you.' And I start running then, because one thing I am, I'm a good runner. I've always had to be with our lot.

Right round the playground she's about an inch behind me but I can hear her breathing and she starts sounding like the pair of bellows Granny Bates has for making her fire go. I think, well, this is it, when one of the teachers comes out into the yard and rings the bell and old Gorilla Face screeches to a halt and yells, 'I'll get you. Just you wait. I'll get you.' Then she runs out of the playground. I thought, that's funny, but then it turns out she doesn't go to our school at all.

We have to line up in the playground before we go into school and I can see old Gorilla Face out of the corner of my eye and she's standing there behind the railings and I think if ever she wore a fur coat, they'd lock her up. Just as we start walking into school though, she shouts, 'I'll be here when you come out, Skinny Lizzie,' and I think the chances of me living long enough to grow up have just about gone altogether.

She's not there at dinner-time, though, and I remember her saying, 'I'll get you tonight,' so I says to our Joe, 'That lass is after me again,' and he says, 'I'll meet you at the gate.' Anyway, comes tea-time and all afternoon I've been in trouble because I couldn't even hear what the teachers were saying, let alone answer their questions, and it's about one minute to four and this teacher suddenly shouts at me, 'And you can stay in. You've not listened to a word all afternoon.' I nearly die. Our Joe has his papers to do and if I'm not out of school dead on four then he'll go without me.

'Please sir,' I say to him. 'I've got to go home because me Granny's died,' and he looks all sorry and says, 'Oh dear, you poor child, you should have said,' and he shouts at the class, 'Why didn't somebody say?' and they all stare at me because they know my Granny died years ago, but none of them says anything to the teacher.

So I get to go home with the rest of the class and there's our Joe waiting for me at the school gate. So is old Gorilla

Face and as soon as she sees me, she starts shouting at me and telling me what I'm going to get and our Joe goes over to her and tells her to take her hook, and she does, but she doesn't go very far and the last I see of her, she's still shouting she's going to get me.

After tea, our Mam says, 'Aren't you going out to play?' and I say, 'I'm not bothered,' and she says, 'I didn't ask you if you were bothered. I asked if you were going out to play.' I say, 'No,' and she says, 'I think you should. It'll do you good after being cooped up all day.' 'I don't mind being cooped up,' I tell her, but she says, 'Well, I do. Here, get your coat on and off you go.'

I don't know why she doesn't just say, 'Go out to play,' instead of asking me if I am or not.

Anyway, I get outside and there's Gorilla Face, standing on the other side of the road and she says, 'Right. Now what are you going to do?' and I think, there's not a lot I can do, so we have a fight and I go back in with half of my hair missing. Our Mam looks at me and says, 'What a mess,' and I say, 'Yes, but you should see what the other one looks like,' and then I start crying and our Mam says, 'I don't know what I'm going to do with you. You're supposed to be growing up a young lady and you're ten times worse than our Joe.'

By the time she's put some ointment on what hair I've got left, I'm feeling terrible and I start coughing and sneezing and she says, 'You're not getting a cold now, are you?' and I get put to bed and I feel rotten.

When our Lucy comes to bed, she says, 'I hear you've been in the wars,' and I say, 'Yes,' and she says, 'Who was it?' and I said, 'She doesn't go to our school, ' and our Lucy says, 'If you see her again when I'm with you, you tell me.' Then our Rose comes in and she says, 'You look better with thin hair anyway,' and I say, 'Oh, thank you very much, I am sure.' Our Lucy says, 'Anyway, our Mam's buying you a new frock tomorrow, isn't she? That'll cheer you up.' I think, oh brother! More trouble, because every time me and our Mam go to get me a new frock, I end up getting sent to bed. Still, because of my sore head, I get to have the feather pillow and even though it's like lying on thin air because all the feathers fly away when you put your head on it, it's a lot better than the hairy one that prickles your cheek.

Chapter Ten

'Why is it wrong to hate our Rose?'

When I got down this morning, our Mam says, 'We're going to buy you a new frock today because we're going to your Aunt's for tea on Sunday and you can't go in that one you've got on. I says, 'Oh! Good,' and our Mam says, 'What's the matter with you? Is that cold still bothering you?' and I say, 'No, Mam. It's gone,' and she says, 'Well, you don't sound very keen,' and I think it's going to be just the same as always and I sneak three of the comics upstairs and put them under my pillow to read when I get sent to bed.

Our Lucy comes in then and she starts telling our Mam all about this picture she saw last night and it's really terrible. 'And he kissed her and she kissed him and they kissed each other, kiss, kiss, kiss,' and I think, ugh! What a rotten old conversation, so I fall down on the floor in a big heap and our Mam jumps up and says, 'Whatever's wrong with you?' and our Lucy says, 'She only does that when she wants some attention, horrible little thing,' so then our Mam rattles me and they go on talking about kiss, kiss, kiss all the time.

I got really fed up, so I stood with my arms up in the air and started going round and round and our Lucy suddenly goes, 'Oh! You frightened me. What are you doing?' and our Mam says, 'For goodness sake, what are you doing now?' I say, 'I'm pretending to be a lighthouse,' and our Mam says, 'A lighthouse?' and our Lucy moans, 'Some lighthouse.' Our Mam says, 'How are you supposed to be a lighthouse?' and I say, 'My smile,' and she says, 'Your what?' and I say, 'My smile. Look, I'm beaming,' and I start smiling with all my teeth again and our Lucy stares at me and says, 'I don't believe it.' Our Joe comes in then and he looks at me and says, 'What's so funny?' and so our Mam tells him I'm pretending to be a lighthouse. Our Joe says, 'She'll never be able to do that,' and I say, 'Why not, clever clogs?' and he says 'Because you're not bright enough,' and then he falls about laughing and so do our Mam and our Lucy.

'Ha, ha,' is all I say.

Anyway, me and our Mam get up town and we go into this shop and I see this beautiful bright pink and black striped frock and I say to our Mam, 'Oh, that's lovely.' Just like that, and she went 'Ugh!' I thought, oh, very nice, so I didn't say anything else. Then she turned round and said, 'You might try and show a bit of interest seeing as how it's for you anyway,' and so then, I have to say, 'Oh, that's nice,' when this woman in the shop brings out this frock which would make a cat sick and they don't even have to wear them.

I scowled at this woman in the shop and she *smiled* back. 'I don't like that,' I says in the end and this woman stops smiling before you can say 'Jack Robinson,' and starts calling our Mam 'Madam' and our Mam starts getting all red and mad like she always does, and we have to come out of the shop so she can tell me off.

I said to her, 'If you'd let me have that pink and black striped one, we could go home,' and she says, 'You'll have that pink and black striped one over my dead body,' and I sigh and she says, 'And stop that everlasting sighing,' and I think, one sigh, and she's going mad.

So, we go into the next shop and in the end, we go into every shop in the town. The trouble is our Mam wants me to wear what she thinks is nice and I think what she thinks is nice is horrible and then she gets mad at me and then I end up with something neither of us likes, and I have this time as well. This frock our Mam buys me is the worst frock I've ever seen in my life. Anyway, we both march home and neither of us says a word and our Mam slams the kettle on the fire when we get in and says, 'That's the last time, young woman, I'm ever going with you for a frock,' and I think I'd better keep quiet and then our Lucy says, 'I'll take her next time, if you like, Mam,' and I think for the very first time in the entire history of the world that it might be all right having our Lucy for a sister because at least she'd be better than our Mam when it came to buying frocks.

I say to her, 'Pity you couldn't have thought of that before,' and she says, 'I'm glad I didn't.' So you see, it doesn't pay to think nice things about people too soon. Our Mam always says, 'A leopard never changes its spots,' and she's right.

And then our Mam looks at me and says, 'I think you'd better go to bed and calm yourself down,' and I thought, thank goodness I put those comics under the pillow, so I trudge upstairs and get into bed and feel under the pillow and they've gone. Somebody's swiped my comics. I just lie there and I think how fed up I am with everything when suddenly the door creaks open and this dirty hand appears waving these comics in the air so I get out of bed and take them and our Joe whispers, 'I only borrowed them. I knew you'd get sent to bed so I've brought them back,' and then he went downstairs and although every step on our stairs creak, I never heard a single sound. Neither did I hear the door open at the bottom either, but then, of course, our Joe is training to be a commando when he grows up so it's only to be expected. I mean, if everybody could hear you coming, they'd shoot you, wouldn't they?

By the time our Mam thought I'd calmed down enough to be let up, it was nearly dinner-time and Mrs Elston from next door came round and asked me if I would just run up to the fish shop for her for some wet fish. I said, 'Yes, Mrs Elston,' because you haven't got any choice. If they ask you, you have to say 'Yes' because if you don't they tell your Mam and then you get into real trouble.

When I came back, she'd been sat talking to our Mam about my new frock and she said to me, 'I've got just the thing for you, young lady. You come round with me. Our Rita used to wear it when she was your age,' and I thought about Mrs Elston's Rita who's quite old – she's got a little girl of her own – and I said, 'Oh, it's all right, Mrs Elston, honest. I love the frock I've got,' and she just smiled and said, 'No, you come along with me.' So I went with her. She went upstairs while I waited in the kitchen and Mr Elston was sat looking into the fire and puffing at his pipe. I thought he hadn't seen me when all of a sudden he says, 'Did you know my thumb comes off?' and I says, 'What? What?' and he says, 'My thumb. I can take it off,' and I says, 'You can't,' and he says, 'I can,' and then Mrs Elston came back downstairs. Over her arm, she had this lovely white frock and it was ever so pretty. 'Here you are,' she says. 'You go home and try this on and if it fits you, you can keep it.'

So I stood there and Mrs Elston looked at me and then at the frock and it was ever so quiet and then she says, 'Er, have you forgotten something?' and I said, 'No,' and she said, 'Oh,' and then Mr Elston said, 'She wants to see me take my thumb off.' Mrs Elston says, 'Oh, Alfred! ' and then Mr Elston took his thumb off and held it up in the air in his other hand and I said, 'That's clever,' and when I got in, I told our Dad about it and our Dad said, 'Look, I'll take mine off for you as well!' and he did.

I says to our Mam, 'Did you know men can take their thumbs off?' and our Mam says, 'What?' and I says to her, 'Can you take your thumb off?' and she says, 'No,' and then our Dad said, 'I'll show you how to do it, look,' and he did and when our Joe came in I said to him, 'Can you take your thumb off?' and he said, 'You're crackers, you are,' and I said, 'I can take mine off,' and I did and he said, 'That's good. Now try it with your head.'

He thinks he's so funny.

I said to him, 'I bet I can stop you laughing,' and he says, 'You'll have a job. Every time I look at you, you make me laugh,' so I says to our Mam, 'Mam, why can't our Joe come with us to that aunt's for tea on Sunday?' and our Mam looked at me and she said, 'Well, I suppose he ought to really,' and you should have seen how fast our Joe stopped laughing then.

'Here,' he says. 'I did you a favour with those comics,' and I thought a bit and said, 'Oh, all right,' and so I never said anything else about our Joe coming with us on Sunday. After all, they only show you up, lads do.

Our Mam says to me, 'Try that frock on then,' and I did and it was about three miles too long and when our Rose came in and saw it, she said, 'I'd like that, Mam,' and our Mam said, 'Well, it is too big for madam here.' I looked at all the white frills round the bottom of the frock and I said, 'She can't have it. It's mine,' and our Mam looked at me and said, 'But you can't wear it. It's too big for you,' and I said, 'I don't care. I don't want our Rose to wear it either.'

Our Mam said, 'That'll do,' and she was really mad and she made me take the frock off and she gave it to our Rose. 'You can have it,' she said and then she said to me, 'You should never let things stand idle,' and I said, 'It won't be standing idle. I'll look at it and then when I'm big enough, I'll wear it.' But our Mam said, no, our Rose had to have it and I said to our Rose, 'I hate you, I do,' and our Rose said, 'Tell me something new.' She rushed upstairs and came down with it on. It was floating all round her legs and the little puff sleeves looked lovely.

I said to her, 'You look horrible in it, you do,' and our Mam said, 'That'll be enough out of you, madam. Our Rose looks lovely in that frock. Now just say you're sorry to her. Being like that with your own sister! I never did.'

It nearly killed me saying I was sorry. I thought I'd choke. Our Rose went smirk, smirk, and she said, 'Let that be a lesson to you,' because she knows how I hate saying I'm sorry when I'm not, and she knew I wasn't. Life's one big lesson, if you ask me. I just wish it would teach me something nice for a change.

Anyway, on Sunday I put on this frock our Mam bought me, which I don't like and our Mam doesn't like, and our Mam went, 'Tsk, tsk!' and sighed. We went to that aunt's for tea and I hope I never see her again as long as I live. It was horrible. We got there and I've only seen her once before and she looks at us and says, 'Tea's on the table.' Our Mam gets into a fluster because she hasn't had time to pull herself together and find out where she is and we get rushed into the front room and sat down at the table and a bowl of jelly's put in front of us before you can blink.

'I don't like jelly,' I say to this aunt, and she looks at me and says, 'Eat it.' So I say again, 'I don't like it,' and she says, 'Eat it' again. Our Mam says, 'She never eats jelly,' and this aunt sniffs and says, 'Waste of good food,' and grabs the bowl and it spills all down my new frock.

'Oh dear,' she says. 'I am sorry.' But she doesn't sound it and I jump up because all the sticky coloured water that's come out of the jelly is going right through my frock and our Mam says, 'Have you got a cloth?' and I drop my skirt and all the jelly falls on to the carpet. You'd think I emptied our dustbin on her carpet the way she carries on. 'Oh dear, ' she says, 'Oh dear! Oh! Screech, screech, screech.' And she's on her hands and knees wiping up this jelly.

I sat down and didn't see our Mam had moved the chair, so I sat down and there was no chair. I fell and my feet catch this Aunt in the bottom as she's bending down, and she whips round and clouts me right across the head before I can do anything. Our Mam nearly has three fits because she's *always* going on about people who hit other people on the head and how they ought to be locked up because you don't know what damage they might do. I sit there on the floor and there's all bells ringing in my head and I start crying and our Mam drags me to my feet and starts shouting at this aunt and finally we end up walking out of the house and marching home.

'That were quick,' our Dad says when we get in and then our Mam starts crying, so do I as well, and she tells our Dad about it all. Our Dad says, 'I told you to keep away,' and then I get sent out to play and our Dad makes a nice hot cup of tea and I hope I never have to see that aunt again as long as I live. So does our Mam.

I had to have a bath before I went to bed because all my legs were sticky with that horrible jelly juice. Our Mam gets the bath out and fills the copper and before you know where you are, everybody wants a bath and people keep coming and saying, 'I'll have one after our Pete, Mam,' and, 'I'll have one after our Lucy, Mam,' and, 'I'll have one after our Rose, Mam' and so that's the bath out for the night, isn't it? And I was going to sit in it and read my comics and Mam was going to make up the fire.

Anyway, I get in the bath and our Mam pokes the fire and it's red hot and lovely and I sit and read my comic for a bit and then I have to get out because everybody else wants to come in.

When it comes to emptying the bath and putting it away, I say to our lads and Lucy and Rose, 'I'll do your share of emptying for a penny a bucket,' and they all moan and groan and then say, 'Oh, all right,' so I earn quite a bit that way until our Mam finds out what I'm charging them and says, 'You ought to have charged them twopence, idle things,' so I say that next time it'll be twopence a bucket and everybody says in that case they'll do it themselves.

'Priced yourself out of the market, have you?' our Mam asks, and she laughs. I say to her, 'You told me to charge them twopence and now they won't let me do any of it.' 'If I told you to put your hand in the fire, our Mam says, 'would you do it?' ''Course I wouldn't,' I say and she says, 'Well then, use a bit of common sense before you do anything anybody tells you to do,' and I nod and think, well, that's one way of getting out of it, to make out it's all my fault for listening to her in the first place, and I think that I'll start deciding things for myself now, seeing as how our Mam lost me my whole entire bucket trade.

When I was hanging the bath up on its nail in the yard, I heard all this noise in the street and our Mam says, 'Whatever's going on?' and I went rushing down the passage and there, walking down the street is a sailor. Not a make believe one but a real, live sailor and he had a navy blue uniform on with bits of white stuck all over it and he looked smashing.

Our Mam said, 'Well, would you ever!' and all the grown-ups in the street rushed out and they were shaking this sailor's hand and slapping his back and everything.

I says to our Mam, 'Who's that, Mam?' and our Mam says, 'It's Mr Wallop,' and I said, 'Teeny's Dad?' and she says, 'Yes. He's been away at sea for a long, long time.' Teeny's Dad, I couldn't help noticing, was pushing a bike. It was a big shiny one with a bell on it and when Teeny got hold of it, she spent the entire night ringing it until her Mam said she'd slap her legs if she didn't stop because it was enough to give you a splitting headache, so it was.

I can't wait till tomorrow to see what else Mr Wallop has brought and if he's still wearing his lovely sailor suit. I says to our Dad, 'Why couldn't you be a sailor?' and he says, 'Because I was a soldier.' I says, 'Soldiers don't look as nice as sailors,' and he said, 'You'll have to marry one then when you grow up,' and that nearly made me sick.

I said to him, 'I'm not going to get married,' and he said, 'What are you going to do then? Stay at home with me and your Mam?' and I said, 'No. I'm going round the world. I might even be a sailor myself,' and our Dad said, was I sure the world was big enough for me because there were times when he doubted it.

Roll on the morning. Teeny said her Dad was going to bring her a camel but I couldn't see one with him tonight. Perhaps the postman will bring it in a van.

Chapter Eleven

'Doesn't the Killer Kid like our Tone?'

WELL, WE ALL RUSHED OUT this morning to see if we could see the sailor again, but Teeny said he wasn't up yet because he'd travelled all round the world yesterday so he was very tired. I said to Teeny, 'Did he bring a camel back with him, then?' and she said, 'Yes,' and I said, 'Where is it then? Have you put it in your back yard?' and she said, 'No, stupid, it's in the front room,' and I said to her, 'Won't it be a bit crowded?' and she said, 'Why?' and I said, 'Well, they look pretty big, camels, when you see their pictures in books.' So that stupid Teeny started shouting and laughing and saying, 'Stupid! Stupid! Skinny Lizzie thinks our Dad brought home a real live camel,' and I said, 'Hasn't he?' and she said, 'Of course he hasn't. What would we do with a real live camel?' I said to her, 'You said he was bringing a camel home, you great fat fibber,' and she says, 'Say that again and

I'll bash you,' and I said, 'You do and I'll tell our Joe.' She's sweet on our Joe so I knew she wouldn't hit me in case our Joe hated her. He does anyway but she pretends he doesn't. 'It's a model,' she says. 'Do you want to look at it?' and I says, 'I'd rather look at a junk yard, thank you very much,' although I was dying to see it. 'Please yourself,' Teeny said and then our Joe came out.

'Do you want a ride on my new bike?' Teeny says to him and she's smiling and batting her eyelashes about a hundred times a second and I can see our Joe go a bit white because I know he can't ride a bike. But all the other kids in the street were wanting a ride on Teeny's bike and she says, 'Nobody can have a ride except Joe Hall,' and our Joe looked as if he'd like to fall down a hole in the ground.

Anyway, our Joe stands there and says, 'I don't want a ride on your old bike,' and then one of his mates starts shouting that he can't ride a bike so I said, 'He can then. He can ride a bike. I seen him ride backwards once and I seen him ride on only one wheel,' and then his mates started laughing and saying, 'He's got to have a little lass to stick up for him,' and our Joe rattled me and then he grabbed Teeny's bike and jumped on it and I didn't breathe until I made him fall off.

I had to make him fall off because I knew he'd fall off anyway with him not being able to ride one so I ran right in front of him and he falls off and lays in the road shouting, 'Now see what you've done! Made me fall off,' and I can see he's right glad, but so's the others won't see I start crying and then our Mam comes rushing out and picks us both up and makes us go in the house. So now me and our Joe are wondering how he can get to learn to ride a bike before he has to go out again.

'Ask our Pete,' I says to him and he tells me to shut up and what do I know about anything so I say, 'Oh, very nice, after falling down for you and scraping all my leg,' and he says,

'Never asked you to, did I?' But he grins at me, so that's all right.

Anyway, our Pete comes home for his dinner and our Joe says to him that he can't ride a bike and all the kids will laugh at him and our Pete says, 'Leave it to me,' and that we had to stay in this afternoon. So we did and when our Pete came home on the tractor, there was this old bike on the back of it and he brought it straight down the passage and into the kitchen. It was a great big bike and our Joe could hardly get on it. 'Here, what're you doing?' our Mam says when she comes into the kitchen and finds our Pete wheeling our Joe round and round. So, we had to tell our Mam and she says, 'Well, we'd better clear the kitchen then so he's got a bit more space,' and our Joe fell off the bike again in surprise because he expected our Mam to go up in the air because she'd just washed and scrubbed the kitchen floor.

Anyway, we moved all the furniture and our Joe started riding round and round the kitchen with our Pete holding on to him and then he did a bit on his own and after hours and hours, he was riding round and round on his own. Then he thumps our Pete on the back and says, 'Thanks, Pete,' and our Pete thumps him on the back and says, 'It's all right, kid,' and I'm sitting there thinking, if they hit each other that hard when they like each other, how hard do they hit when they don't like each other?

'What about me?' I said and our Pete looks at me as if I've just crawled out from under a stone and says, 'You?' and I says, 'Yes. I can't ride a bike either,' and he moans and groans and then he says, 'Our Joe can teach you now,' and our Joe looks at me and then at the bike and I hold my leg and start going, 'Oooooh! Ooooh! That hurts, that does,' and he says, 'Oh, blooming heck! All right then Come on.' And so I get on the bike and he rides me round the kitchen.

Then, just when I'm sat up in the air feeling good, I find

I'm looking at our Joe and I say to him, 'How can I be looking at you when you should be behind me, holding the bike?' and he says 'You're on your own now, look. You can ride.' And I fell off.

And I landed flat on our Joe and he's lying there on the floor saying, 'What did you do that for?' and I say to him, 'Because you let go. You're not supposed to let go,' and he says, ''Course I'm supposed to let go, you big dope,' and I say to him, 'But you didn't *tell* me you were going to let go,' and in the end, he says, 'Well, that's all the lesson you're getting, because I'm going out now to practise,' and he went.

Our Mam came into the kitchen and she said, 'Do you want to help me get it straight again?' and I say, 'No. I want to go with our Joe,' and she says, 'Well, you can't. You've got to help me straighten up this kitchen,' and I say to her, 'Why do you always ask me if I want to do something and then when I say 'No,' tell me I've got to do it?' and she says, 'Because you always give the wrong answer, that's why.' So what do you make of that?

Our Joe got to keep the bike. Our Pete bought it for him. It only cost him three shillings because the farmer said it was no good but after our Pete had fixed the brakes, it was O.K.

He said to our Joe, 'I've fixed the brakes, so you'll be all right now,' and our Joe goes into the street and we're all standing at the front door watching him. He comes belting down the street doing about a hundred miles an hour and then he puts the brakes on and he flys right over the handlebars and ends up in a big heap on the road – *again*.

'Oh! Oh!' shouts our Mam. 'Are you all right, Joe?' and our Pete stands there laughing his head off. 'I see the brakes are working O.K. Joe,' he says and he goes off back in the house and he's still laughing half an hour later when our Joe is being bandaged up because he's in a right state.

'Oh, very funny,' our Joe shouts at last and then our Pete

says, 'Never mind, kid. At least you can ride a bike now and nobody else saw you come off it but us.'

I asked our Pete if he could get me a bike but our Mam came in and she put her hand to her head and said to our Pete, 'Don't you dare bring her a bike home. It makes me feel poorly to even think of her on a bike,' and our Pete says, 'I wasn't going to,' which I think is very unfair because now I've had to arrange with our Joe to pay a penny a ride so I'm going to be paying for rides all the time from now on. I shall have a bike when I grow up and I shall ride it everywhere.

The worst thing of all is that our Joe can get away from me so easy now because he gets on his bike and he's gone in a flash. He used to try and get rid of me by running before, but I can run nearly as fast as him so that didn't work. Well, I shall just have to learn to run faster. Boys have all the fun.

Because I'd covered up for our Joe when he fell off Teeny Wallop's bike, he says to me, 'Do you want to come with me to see our Tone box the Killer Kid?' I nearly fainted with shock and I said, 'Oh yes, please,' before he could change his mind and he said, 'You'll sit there and be quiet, won't you?' and I said, 'Yes,' and he said, 'Because I'm telling you, one word and you're out on your ear,' and I said, 'I shan't hardly breathe,' so in the end he says, 'Come on then, and don't tell our Mam.'

As if I would! I know what our Mam would say. She'd go 'Oh! Oh! It's wicked it is, boxing. Wicked.' But then our Mam thinks it's wicked if two butterflies bump into each other, and she's saying things like, 'Oh, those poor butterflies,' and as for ladybirds, well! We have to look at every piece of washing when we fetch it in in the summer in case there are any ladybirds on it and when our Mam finds one she holds it out and tells it to fly home because its poor little house is on fire and its poor little kids have all gone. I says to her, 'You must be giving that ladybird a heart attack,

Mam,' and she says, 'I'm not. That's just to make it fly home.' I says to her, 'Not much point in it going home if its kids have all gone and its poor little house is all on fire,' and our Mam looks at me and I think, aren't Mams queer, and wonder if everybody has the same trouble with their Mam as we do with ours.

So, our Joe took me up to see our Tone boxing this other lad. They were in this square and it was called a ring and it wasn't a ring at all. I said to our Joe, 'That's not a ring, that's a square,' and he said, 'Are you going to be quiet or shall I send you home?' and I said, 'Oh, all right, I'll be quiet.'

This other lad in the ring (square) with our Tone looks ever so fierce and he's got something wrong with his mouth. I says to our Joe, 'Is that the Killer Kid?' and our Joe says, 'Yes, now shut up,' and I say, 'What's wrong with his mouth?' because it was all bulging out and our Joe says, 'There nothing wrong with *his* mouth. It's *your* mouth that's the trouble.' I says to our Joe, 'My mouth doesn't stick out like that,' and he says, 'Neither does his, stupid. He's wearing a gum shield.' 'What's that for?' I say, and our Joe says it's to stop all their teeth getting bashed out. I think boxing can't be very good after all. I says to our Joe, 'Has our Tone got one of them, then?' and our Joe says, 'Yes, and one more word out of you and out you go.' So I just hope our Tone has got one because what our Mam would say if he came home without any teeth, I just don't know.

Then this lad and our Tone walk into the middle of the square ring and touch each other's gloves and then walk back to their corners (and that proves it's not a ring because rings don't *have* corners) and then this man rings this bell and our Tone and this lad rush out of their corners and start thumping each other.

'They're hitting each other very hard,' I says to our Joe and he says, 'That's what they're supposed to do,' and I says,

'But that lad's hitting our Tone more than our Tone's hitting him,' and our Joe shakes his head and says, 'He is, isn't he?' and I says to him, 'Well, you can sit here if you like but I'm going to help our Tone.'

I ran down to the ring and I tripped that lad up when he came near me and then I shouted to our Tone, 'Hit him now, Tone! Now he's on the floor. Go on, hit him!' And our Tone says, 'You little devil ! Gerrof home!' and he starts shouting our Joe, 'Joe! Joe! Come and get this kid before I murder her,' and I think, don't bother to say thank you.

So our Joe drags me home and hits me all the way there. So I kick him and hit him back because I'm not going to be like our Tone and let anybody hit me more than I hit them.

Our Joe tells me not to say anything to our Mam but when we get in he's still so mad that he's stamping round the kitchen snarling at me all the time until our Mam says, 'What on earth?' and then our Joe tells her everything. She says to me, 'You keep away from there. Little girls aren't supposed to go in there,' and she tells our Joe he's never to take me in that place again.

Then our stupid Tone comes in and I says to him, 'Why didn't you hit that lad when he was on the floor?' and he starts shouting and yelling at me as well and saying, 'That were only the Killer Kid you tripped up, I suppose you know, I'll never be able to show my face in there again. For two pins I'd take you upstairs and drop you out of the bedroom window!' So our Mam says to him, 'She were only trying to help,' and I says, 'I was. Now I wish I'd tripped you up instead,' and our Tone says, 'Oh, well, all right, but don't do it again, that's all.' I say to him, 'What's a cauliflower ear?' and he sighs and says, 'Roll on the day she leaves home,' and I think, oh yes, very nice.

Anyway, our Tone had beat the Killer Kid so he's feeling very pleased with himself. He starts dancing around telling us he's shadow boxing. 'What's shadow boxing?' I say to him and he says, 'It's boxing somebody who isn't there,' and I look at him and he looks at me and I say, 'If he isn't there, how can you see when he's going to hit you?' and our Tone stops dead and starts going, 'Oh! Oh! You're so stupid, you are,' and I say to him, 'It's not me what's stupid. I don't hit people who aren't there. Not till I can see them anyway,' and our Mam says, 'That'll do.'

Our Tone turns round and looks at our Mam, sat in her chair, and he says to her, 'Don't move, Mam.' So our Mam trys to get out of the chair because I can see she's thinking, what's he going to do? But she's too late and our Tone lifts the chair and our Mam right up to the ceiling and our Mam's shouting blue murder.

Our Dad comes rushing down the stairs and the stair door flies open and hits our Tone and there's this chair, with our Mam in it, wobbling about up on the ceiling.

'Put me down,' she's shouting. Our Tone stands there and turns round to our Dad and says, 'That hurt my back, that door. You should be more careful.' Our Dad looks round the kitchen and then he looks up at the chair and says, 'What are you doing with your mother?' and our Tone says, 'Nobody can take a joke in this house,' and he brings the chair down and our Mam jumps out of it and starts running him round the room and in the end our Tone has to run into the yard, because our Mam is really mad.

'Just you wait till I get my hands on you,' she's shouting and our Tone's laughing that much, he can hardly run, so our Mam catches him and when she trys to clout him, our Tone holds her hands and she's dancing about and getting madder and madder. Anyway, in the end, he lets her go and he runs like mad and our Mam comes back into the kitchen and says, 'To think you can't even sit down in peace any more,' and I have to make her a cup of tea to get over the shock. 'Put plenty of sugar in,' she says, so I do and then get told off because I used too much.

Granny Bates and Old Flo and Mrs Elston come round to find out what all the shouting's about and our Mam tells them and Old Flo says 'It's a blessing he never did that to me,' and tells our Mam it's a good job she's only a young woman. 'Young!' our Mam says. 'I stand need to be young! They've aged me twenty years, this bunch has just lately,' and Granny Bates and Old Flo and Mrs Elston all nod their heads and look at me (who hasn't done a thing) and say, 'Yes, we know what you mean.'

'Never mind,' Granny Bates says, 'they'll all leave home one day,' and our Mam says, 'Oh well, they're not all that bad, you know,' and I think I'm glad our Mam's our Mam and not Granny Bates because Granny Bates would probably pack our bags for us and show us where the front door was as soon as we left school. 'Cheerio!' she'd say and you'd say, 'See you soon,' and she'd say, 'Not if I see you first,' because she's always saying, 'Birds have always got to leave the nest.'

I saw a picture once of a bird kicking one of its own little birds out of its nest. It was a good job the little bird learnt how to fly on the way down because the nest was a long way up.

I think, at least our Mam'll give us a parachute when she kicks us out.

Chapter Twelve

'What does our Pete want to marry Miss Brown for anyway?'

IT WAS FUNNY Granny Bates saying that we'd all be leaving home one day, because I ran away last night with a handkerchief tied on the end of a stick like Dick Whittington. But our Dad found me and brought me back.

It's Miss Brown, you see. The dancing teacher. Our Pete's been courting her, and me and Miss Brown don't like each other and our Pete told our Mam that he and Miss Brown were going to get engaged.

Our Mam said, 'But you're too young to get engaged,' and our Pete says, 'I shall be eighteen next month and I want to get engaged to Ruby before I go to do my National Service.'

So I'm sat there thinking about our Pete marrying Miss Brown and I say to him, 'Couldn't you have picked somebody better than her.' I thought he was going to explode he went that red. Our Mam said, 'You watch your tongue, young lady, and don't be so rude.' So I went out, because I don't mind our Pete at all but I don't like Miss Brown one little bit.

Last time I was at dancing class, Miss Brown said to me, 'You're very self-willed for your age,' and I said to her, 'What does that mean?' and she said, 'Spoilt.' I looked at her and said, 'I'm not spoilt,' because Gloria Hottentot is spoilt, and if I'm like her I might as well throw myself in the canal because she is just plain horrible.

Miss Brown says, 'Well, all I can say is that you've got a lot to say for yourself. Personally, I think you ought to be checked more often,' and all this just because I wouldn't balance a glass of water on my head and go through a hoop at the same time.

I said to her, 'I'm not a performing seal, you know,' and she said, 'How dare you, you horrible little girl? If I can do it, so can you. It's for the concert and if you want to be in it, you have to learn how to do acrobatics and this is what everyone else will be doing.'

I said, 'I can't see the point in balancing a glass of water on my head and going through a hoop,' and she said, 'I think you'd better stop coming to my classes.' I said, 'All right,' and packed up my things ready to go home.

Miss Brown pretended to ignore me but I could see she kept looking at me when she thought I wasn't looking at her and she said in a loud voice, 'Now, class. I know there are some people who can't do a perfectly simple exercise but I'm sure the rest of you intelligent girls will be able to do it without any trouble at all,' and she put this glass of water on her forehead and started going slowly down to the floor, backwards. Then she whipped this rotten old hoop over her head and started sliding through it somehow and although I know I shouldn't have done it, I couldn't help myself, and I stamped on the floor and the glass of water fell off Miss Brown's forehead and she was going, 'Urgle-gurgle! Ugh! Ugh! Wait till I get hold of you!' She got all tangled up in her hoop she was in such a hurry to get her hands on me. I didn't wait to see what would happen when she did get herself sorted out. I ran home.

When I got in, though, I had to tell our Mam everything that had happened and she said, 'You're a shame and disgrace,' and she was just going on to, 'You'll have to see your father,' when there was this loud banging on our front door and when our Mam went it was Miss Brown on the doorstep and all her hair was dripping water and she looked mad enough to split me straight in two.

'I've come to see about your daughter,' she went, without hardly opening her mouth either and our Mam said, 'Come in, Ruby. I've heard all about it and you can take it from me that that young madam will be sorry she's played you up tonight. She's going to see her father when he comes in,' and our Mam turns round and stares at me as hard as she can.

She says, 'Say you're sorry to Miss Brown,' and I daren't say I won't so I don't say anything and I can *feel* our Mam getting madder and madder and she says again, 'Say you're sorry to Miss Brown,' and I shake my head and our Mam slaps me very hard and tells me I'm to go to bed.

It didn't half hurt, the slap, but I think I'll turn into a tree before I cry in front of Miss Brown, so I walk ever so slowly out of the room and open the stairs door and go upstairs. When I get to the top though I creep back down and sit behind the door and listen.

Miss Brown's saying, 'It's a shame we can't get on because she's a good dancer,' and our Mam's saying, 'Yes, well, it's just one of those things. She won't be coming any more, of course,' and then Miss Brown goes, 'Oh' – cough, cough. 'Oh, I do hope this won't put you off Peter and I getting engaged, Mrs Hall,' and our Mam says she doesn't really think it's a very good idea but then, there are two years and if anybody changes their mind, well, they can, can't they, and no harm done. Miss Brown goes, 'Yes, yes, yes,' and she says, 'If we did get married, though, I would have liked . . . your daughter . . . to have been a bridesmaid at the wedding,' and I think, I'll be a bridesmaid over my dead body, and then I hear our Dad coming in.

Anyway, I got a real telling off from our Dad and our Mam and me had this talk about Manners Maketh Man. I didn't do much talking. Our Mam did it all and she said if ever I was so rude to someone older than me again, then she'd threat, threat, threat, and not only that but she'd warn, warn, warn, until in the end, I decided never to speak again just to be on the safe side.

I know one thing, though. I hate Miss Brown.

Our Pete kept saying that I should say I was sorry to her and he kept on and on about it but our Mam said, 'No good will come of madam here and Ruby meeting again. Not for a while anyway.' But our Pete kept going on about it until last night when he brought Miss Brown round to the house and she sat there and I sat there and our Mam says to me, 'Do you want to apologise to Miss Brown for being so rude, now you've had time to think about it?' and I shook my head. So our Mam said, 'Perhaps you'd better go and think about it some more upstairs,' and Miss Brown stared at the mantelpiece with her lips all tight across her face. I says to our Mam, 'But she was ever so rude to me as well, Mam,' but our Mam just waved in the air at me and so I went.

When I got upstairs though, I thought, I'm not having this, so I crept back down and got some bread and lard out of the pantry and wrapped it up in a paper bag and filled a pop bottle full of water and then I went back upstairs and took one of our Dad's hankies and put my bread and lard in that. Then I put in all these pages I've written on and a pencil, and then I put in a candle, and three pennies I had that Old Flo gave me for going right to the top of the town for her yesterday. She wanted some fish and I had to queue for about nineteen hours to get it for her and when I got back she gave me the three pennies. 'You're a good lass,' she said and all I'm glad is that there's *somebody* who likes me.

Then I dropped out of our bedroom window and I started walking. It was freezing cold and it was ever so dark and as soon as I got out of the streets, I was scared to death. I walked and walked and walked and it started snowing and I thought, oh, thanks very much. That's all I need.

When I couldn't walk any farther, I went and laid down in the bottom of a hedge because it was a bit warmer there and I thought, what I need here is a few leaves, but there weren't any. I should have run away in the summer. It would have been a lot better to run away in the summer and I thought, I wish I'd waited.

Then I was going to light the candle but I couldn't see where I'd put our Dad's hankie because it was that dark, so I had to crawl out of the hedge to find it and when I found it, I hadn't got a match to light it with anyway so I was as bad burnt as scalded, as our Mam says, though why, I don't know. It wasn't very nice there and I didn't stop long. I thought, I don't reckon much to this, and I got out from the hedge and started to walk back home.

The sky was as black as anything and I looked at the stars and I thought, I hope they're stuck on all right, because the last thing I wanted was a star falling on my head. Anyway, I only saw one star fall and I walked with my head back so I could keep an eye on where it had gone after that. I wanted to make sure it didn't turn round in the sky and come and get me.

The Sunday School teacher once said to me, 'those stars

you see falling out of the sky are little angels come back to earth,' and I said, 'Gerrof,' and she said, 'It's true,' and I said, 'Talk about lies.' 'I'm not telling lies,' she said. 'Have you seen one then?' I asked her. 'Have you ever seen a star fall and an angel get up out of its place?' And she shook her head, and I said, 'No, and you never will because when that Micky jumped off the cliff, he got a broken leg and a broken arm and he didn't jump out of no heaven either. So, any angel that jumped out of heaven would be smashed to little bits when it landed, wouldn't it?' And the Sunday School teacher looked at me and said, 'Oh ye of little faith,' and I said, 'You'll be telling us next they've got wings and they keep them folded under their shirts and their frocks,' and I went home because I don't think Sunday School teachers should tell lies. It's bad enough us doing it, without them starting as well.

Well, I was keeping an eye on that star and the next minute I find myself lying in a big heap on the pavement and everything's going round and I think, oh heck, that star got me after all. Then I don't remember anything else until I find myself lying in my own bed (well, my own and Lucy's and Rose's bed).

'What happened?' I says to our Mam and she says, 'You walked into a lamp post,' and I mutter, 'Think that if you like but I know it was that star that got me. Some angel, landing on people's heads and flattening them. Just wait till I see that Sunday School teacher again.'

Anyway, Miss Brown comes round the bedroom door and I says to our Mam, 'Oh heck, Mam, I'm not going to say I'm sorry,' and Miss Brown says, 'I'm sorry,' and I think I must be dying. So I shout at our Mam, 'Here, Mam, I'm not dying, am I?' and she says, 'Don't be daft. Why should you be dying?' and I say, 'Because Miss Brown's said she's sorry.' 'And you should do the same,' our Mam says.

So I say, 'I'm sorry too,' and Miss Brown smiles and says, 'I've brought you some sweets,' and I say, 'No thanks,' and our Mam bashes my leg, so I have to smile and say, 'Oh, thank you very much.' She goes away then, thank goodness.

The only funny thing is that it's daytime and I can't remember the night going. Everybody keeps tiptoeing around and that nice doctor with the cool hands came to see me again this morning.

'What are we going to do with you?' he says and pats my head and I thought it was going to fall off because it hurts ever so much.

'Ouch!' I says and he says, 'Ooops, sorry!' and I think, oh, grown-ups, you can do nothing with them at all.

Miss Brown comes to see me about three more times and the first time she comes she says, 'Can't we start again? After all, if I'm going to be in the family . . .' and I think, 'Oh, not that,' and she goes on, 'If I'm going to be in the family, we really ought to try and get on with each other,' so I say, 'If you like,' and she snaps, 'Oh, don't go mad, will you?' and that was the end of being friends for that night.

I wish I could like her because our Pete hardly ever speaks to me these days. He just glares at me and keeps saying, 'You're just plain bad, you are,' and I don't say anything because after our Mam warned me about Manners Maketh-ing Man I think probably it's better to keep quiet for a bit.

Our Mam says, 'Why don't you like her?' and I says, 'I don't know,' and then our Mam gets mad with me all over again.

Today though, they brought our Pete home in an ambulance and our Mam was as white as a sheet and Old Flo and Granny Bates and Mrs Elston were walking ever so quietly around the house. They sent for our Dad from work and when he got in he says, 'Which one of them is it?' because he didn't know if it was our Pete in an accident at the farm or our Tone in an accident at the pit but it was our Pete. All the roads and fields and everything were covered in snow and it was icy cold and our Pete had been out on his tractor and it had turned over and trapped him underneath it.

I got under the table with our Prince because it was terrible in our house. Our Mam wasn't crying or anything but she couldn't speak until our Pete was tucked up in bed and the doctor had told her that he hadn't done anything serious, because luckily the tractor had only caught one of his legs and then our Mam went, 'Oh!' and fell in a big heap on the floor. Me and our Prince sat and cried together. Our Prince always cries when I do, just like I always cry when our Mam does.

Anyway, when Mrs Elston and Old Flo and Granny Bates had picked our Mam up and she'd come round, they all trooped upstairs to see our Pete and I heard the front door open and then I heard this, 'Oh dear!' – sob, sob, sob – and I pushed the tablecloth up and there was Miss Brown and she was crying buckets and I said to her, 'Do you want to come under here with me?' and she said, 'Yes,' and she crawled under the table with me and I put my arm round her, and our Prince put his paw on her knee and we all sat and cried. Of course, our Prince doesn't cry tears which is just as well otherwise we'd have needed a boat to get out from under there in the end.

Then our Mam comes downstairs with Old Flo and Mrs Elston and Granny Bates and I hear our Mam say, 'Whatever's that noise?' and of course that noise was me and our Prince and Miss Brown, and our Mam lifted the tablecloth up and she said, 'Oh, you poor thing,' and held out her arms and helped Miss Brown out! I thought, oh yes, very nice, so I stayed where I was and our Mam told Granny Bates to take Miss Brown up to our Pete and to sit with them while they had a little talk.

Then our Mam got me out and I sat on her knee and she said our Pete was quite all right now and I was very glad about that.

'Have you and Miss Brown made friends?' she said and I said, 'Well, I don't like to see anybody cry, Mam,' and our Mam said that wasn't what she asked me so I said, 'I suppose she's all right,' and our Mam said, 'You'll have plenty of time to get to know her better if she's coming into the family.' So I says to her, 'But it won't be long before I'm going out, will it?' and she says, 'Whatever do you mean?' so I told her I was planning to probably go round the world and she said, 'Oh, I see. In that case,' she says, 'you'd better get yourself off to bed. You'll need plenty of sleep to go round the world on.'

Sometimes I think all the days are full of getting up and going to bed and nothing else.

Anyway, now I know our Pete's O.K. I'm looking forward to the morning because our Joe's promised to take me sledging with the snow being so deep. He has to take me because he needs me to push the sledge. I can hardly wait.

Chapter Thirteen

'Why did the coal men swear, Mam?'

It was still snowing this morning when I got up and our Joe had already got the old sledge out. 'Come on,' he says, 'let's go down the hill': so we set off down the hill and I'm on the back because, like I said, I have to do the pushing to get it going because our Joe says I can't steer and if I sit there and he pushes, we'll only end up going into the wall. So, we set off and the sledge goes really fast, about a hundred miles an hour down the hill and this coal lorry pulls out across the road.

Our Joe starts shouting to me to keep my head down and I can see this lorry getting nearer and nearer and the next second, we've gone whizzing underneath it and out the other side and halfway up the other hill before we stop.

We're turning the sledge round to go back down the hill when our Joe says, 'Here, look at them two men,' and we see it's the coal men and they're running up the hill towards us, and they're shouting, 'Little devils. Just you wait till we get our hands on you.' (They were really shouting, little swear words, but I'd better not write them down in case our Mam ever reads this because she'll only say, 'There's never no need to use bad language, no matter what,' and if you say to her, 'But the coal men used it, not me,' she only says, 'Then there's no need for you to set a bad example by repeating it.' So I'll just leave it out.)

Anyway, there they were, coming up the hill like the clappers and our Joe says, 'I think we'd better get out of here,' and we both start running but we can't go very fast because we have to pull the sledge as well and the biggest of the coal men catches hold of my frock and that's it. Our Joe comes back and says to him, 'You let go of her, she's my sister,' and this coal man says, 'I don't care if she's your Granny,' and he tips me up and puts me over his knee and he doesn't half hit me. Our Joe's dancing around and shouting, 'I'm going to fetch our Dad to you,' and this other coal man up-ends him and does the same to him.

This other coal man says, 'You nearly gave me a heart attack, you little . . .' – swear words – and our Joe says, 'You wait till I tell our Dad.' The coal man says, 'I don't feel like waiting. Come on, let's go and find him,' and he asks Joe where we live and Joe says, 'I'm not telling you.' So they march us and the sledge down the hill, and then they stop everybody going down the street and they say, ''Ere, Missis, where do these kids live?' and of course, in the end, they get somebody who tells them. They put us on the back of the lorry and one of the coal men drives the lorry to our house and our Mam comes out and he tells her all about us.

She says, 'I don't think I can stand much more.' Then our Dad comes out, and he's been wakened up because he was in bed after being on nights, and he doesn't look very pleased. When the coal men tell him about us, he says, 'You did right,' and then tells us off.

Our Joe says, 'Aren't you going to hit him, Dad?' and he says, 'The only people who're going to get hit around here are about your size and there's two of them.' So, I whisper to our Joe that it's school time and the last *we* see of them all, they're all stood staring after us in the street.

'All your fault,' our Joe says to me and then he runs off to his mates and I have to go to school on my own.

When we came out of school at dinner-time, I asked our Mam if I could just go to the paper shop and she said, 'Yes, but don't be long.'

It's coming up to Christmas, you see, and I've been hanging my nose over some books the paper shop's had in for weeks and weeks now and hoping I'll get them. Every day I go down and look in the window and every day they're still there. I think I'd probably die if I went down and they'd gone.

There are three of them, these books. They're all about this family of girls who're really poor but do exciting things and everything and one of them wants to be a writer. Just like me. I told our Mam about them and she said, 'There's nothing new under the sun, is there?' and I said to her, 'Oh yes, there is. My writing won't be like her writing and, when I'm rich and famous, I'll buy you a lovely house in the middle of a field, just like you always wanted.' And she said, 'And I supppose if I buy you these books, you'll be able to do that,' and I tried to look really trustworthy and said, 'Yes.' I thought, keep it simple.

Anyway, our Mam smiled but she didn't promise anything. When I grow up, I shall always say, 'Yes, you can have that, that and that,' to my kids. Well, I would have done but I'm not going to have any. And I'm not going to have any because I couldn't stand them if they turned out like our

Pete and Tone and Joe and Lucy and Rose. Ugh! Fancy having to live with them for the rest of your life.

Today was the very last day at school before the Christmas holidays and they let us out of school at half-past three this afternoon. That was good but what wasn't good was that you had to answer a question before you could go. Nearly all the class had gone by the time I got one right and when I got out there's our Lucy and Rose waiting for me.

'Come on,' they said. 'Trust you to be last out. We're going carol singing tonight.'

I love going carol singing more than anything else in the world. We go up to all the posh houses and sometimes they ask us in and sometimes they set the dog on us. It all depends on what they're like. So, we rushed through tea and then we were off.

Our Mam said, 'Don't be late,' and our Lucy and Rose said, 'Oh no, we won't,' knowing very well we'd be out until they thought everyone had gone to bed.

It was thick with snow and besides that it had started snowing again as well. We walked right over to the other end of the town to the posh houses and then our Lucy and Rose pushed me in front and said, 'Come on, we'll start here,' so we stood outside this house and started singing, 'silent night, holy night,' which was a wrong choice for a start because all of a sudden the front door of this house rocked. I thought they had a lion in there. All you could hear was these growls and barks and this great thing kept throwing itself at the door.

'I'm frightened,' I said and turned round and there was nobody there. Our Lucy and Rose were halfway down the street.

I thought, 'Wait till we get home and I tell our Mam, that's all.' I started running down the path and the door opened and I didn't bother stopping to open the gate, I jumped over it. It was ever such a high one as well but you'd have thought I was a deer the way I went over it.

'They've set the dog on me,' I yelled and I was crying and I couldn't see anything. Then our Lucy and Rose suddenly appeared at the side of me and they turned round to the big house and they shouted and yelled at the man who was standing in the door. 'Yer great bully,' they shouted. 'She's only a little kid. If I were a feller,' our Lucy shouted, 'I'd come and bash you, you rotten old thing,' and this man shouted, 'Gerrof, snotty little brats! I'll set the dog on you if you come here again.' Our Rose said, 'We're going to tell our Dad of you. He'll come and sort you out,' and the man shouted, 'Yes, and I'll have the police on him and you as well if you don't take yourselves off. Disturbing people, you nasty mucky little devils!'

I said to our Rose, 'Oh, let's go,' because I was scared to death, honest, but then our Lucy said, 'Look at that,' and I looked up and our Rose looked up and there was this girl standing in the bedroom window and she was laughing. 'She'll laugh on the other side of her face in a minute,' our Rose said happily. 'She goes to our school,' and Rose stood under the lamplight for a second so that the girl could see who she was, and then our Lucy went and stood at the side of her and I was dragged along behind them and laughing girl at the window suddenly looked as sick as a dog.

'There's no school till after Christmas,' our Rose said. 'But never mind. There's all next year,' and both of them grinned and, wonder of wonders, gave me a hand-carry all the way down the street.

When we got home we added up the money we'd earned and it came to sixteen shillings and ninepence and I got five shillings and our Rose five and sixpence and our Lucy got six and threepence.

'Why do they have to have more than me?' I says to our

Mam and our Mam says, 'You ought to share it equally,' to our Lucy and Rose. 'She's done as much work as you have,' our Mam said. So our Lucy and Rose said, 'Here, you can have all the oranges and sweets instead,' and they gave me three oranges and about eight sticky sweets. I didn't reckon much to that but I thought if I made them mad they wouldn't take me with them tomorrow night. Our Mam won't let me go on my own and our Joe goes with the lads so I gave the oranges and sweets to our Mam and she put them in the cupboard for Christmas Day.

Our Mam made some cocoa and poked the fire and we all sat in the firelight drinking our cocoa and telling ghost stories and then our Joe came in and he says, 'There's a ghost lives under the stairs and it only comes out at night and it only goes in the back bedroom.' That's where I sleep and our Mam looks at our Joe and she says, 'If I catch any more ghosts in this house, they'll feel my hand on their legs,' and our Pete laughed and said, 'Ghosts don't have legs.' Our Mam says, 'The ghost I'm thinking of does. In fact, it has six,' and then our Pete and Tone and Joe started spluttering into their cocoa. They think they're so funny. Personally, I think I'd rather live with a ghost than with them.

Perhaps not though.

When I got up in the morning, I had to go and help our Mam make the paper chains. Lick, lick, lick all morning but the chains looked ever so pretty and our Tone put them up. 'Yes, very nice,' our Dad says when he came in and then he walked straight into them and broke one. 'Look what our Dad's done.' I said to our Mam and our Dad says, 'I couldn't help it. They're too low.' So then he hung them up again and they practically vanished into the ceiling. I says to our Mam, 'I hope I get a magnifying glass for Christmas,' and she says, 'Why?' and I says, 'So I can see the trimmings,' and she laughed and said, well, we couldn't have our Dad walking around draped in paper chains all the time, could we? I asked if I could just nip down to the paper shop to see if my books were still there and our Mam said, yes, but don't be long and when I got there, the most terrible thing in my life had happened. I looked in the window and the books had gone!

I said to the girl behind the counter, 'What you done with them books that was in the window?' and she said, 'They've been sold, that's what's been done with them,' and I said to her, 'But you knew I wanted them.' 'I couldn't hold on to them for ever,' she says, all nasty. 'They was there and now they has gone and that is all there is to it.'

'Did our Mam buy them?' I asked, all hope like.

She shook her head. She knows our Mam you see because she only lives round the corner from us. 'She never bought them,' she said, and so here I am and I wish I was dead.

I think I wanted those books more than anything in the world. More than a bike even.

As if that wasn't enough to ruin my entire whole life, our Tone's got himself a girl-friend now and he brought her round again tonight when I was sat looking out of the window thinking what a terrible Christmas it was going to be.

This girl sits down on the sofa and stares at our Mam as if our Mam's got two heads or something. I says to her, 'Do you like books?' and she jumps about three feet in the air and says, 'What? What?' and I say, 'Do you like books?' and she says, 'Depends what you mean by books,' and I look at her and think, what does she mean, it depends what I mean by books? I was just going to ask her when our Tone says, 'Buzz off!' and I think, oh, how polite, and I wonder why this girl goes out with him at all. I reckon there must be something wrong with her.

Our Mam says there doesn't have to be anything wrong with her just because she goes out with our Tone. 'He's a very nice boy,' she says but you can't go by what our Mam says about any of us because she thinks we're all nice. Also, she's not littler than the others, like I am.

We're going to the Sunday School Christmas Party next week, if I live that long. I don't feel very well and our Mam says it's because I'm sickening for a cold. Personally, I think it's because I've got a broken heart through that horrible girl selling my three lovely books.

Chapter Fourteen

'Dad, is it Christmas now?'

I'VE BEEN IN BED a whole week now because I went down with a bad cold and I had to stay at home and all the snow went while I was in bed, so now it's gone and I bet it doesn't come back till next year.

It's a good thing I'm better now, though, because the Sunday School had their Christmas Party last night and me and our Rose had to go to it. Our Rose didn't stay long because she said to our Mam, 'I'm too old for this now, Mam,' and our Mam said, 'All right, you can go.' And she went, so I was there on my own, except for our Mam. All the Mams came. They do every year. They lay out the tables and serve all the kids and everything and then afterwards they sit and have a cup of tea together.

I thought it was going to be a terrible party but it turned

out very good and I was really glad I went, mainly because of the magician. He said he was a magician and he pulled this rabbit out of a hat and dropped it and it ran under the tables and everybody had to get up and look for it. Poor little thing. Nobody found it though, and our Mam said, 'I bet that'll make somebody a good dinner,' and the magician was having a fit. He kept shouting, 'It's got to be here somewhere. Nobody's leaving this hall until I find it,' but after a bit, he had to get on with his show. 'Nobody leaves this hall until it's found,' he kept shouting.

Then he stood there and said, 'And for my next trick, I shall change this plain white handkerchief into a coloured one,' and he starts throwing this white hankie about in the air and catching it and one of the little Berry twins walks up to him and says, 'Here, Mister,' and pulls this coloured hankie from the magician's sleeve. I thought he was going to kill the little twin but he patted its head instead. I don't know which twin it was. There's a boy and a girl but you can't tell which is which because they keep swapping clothes with each other and they both have short yellow hair as well.

Our Mam says, 'I'd make that little madam grow her hair,' and the twin's Mam says, 'I've tried but they cut it off between them,' so our Mam didn't say any more. She just looked at me and said, 'Twins!' as if they'd got the plague or something.

Anyway, this magician stands there and he's trying to smile and he says, 'And now for my next trick, I shall make a bird fly out of my hat,' and our Mam says, 'He wants to watch it don't fly right away, like his rabbit,' and the magician stares round the hall and bends right over his hat and he brings out a little bird. Ever such a pretty bird and he says, 'And now it will sing for you,' and this pretty little bird starts singing and our Mam says, 'That's not a real bird,' and the magician says, 'What do you want for your money. A

Zoo?' Our Mam says, 'Oh! Sorry, I'm sure,' and nobody claps at all because one of the twins shouts, 'There's a little box under your hat, Mister,' and the magician looks as if he's going to cry.

'That's the end of the show,' he says and everybody claps him and starts cheering and he starts smiling then. 'Well,' our Mam says, 'poor bloke. Not much fun losing your rabbit,' and all the Mams are grinning away and the magician starts walking round the hall and crawling on his hands and knees going, 'Tu-tu-tu-tu-tu-tu. Where are you?' Our Mam has a little laugh and then the magician gets up and goes away without his rabbit. 'Shame,' our Mam says.

Then we play musical chairs which is the worst game in the whole wide world. Miss Plum sits at the piano and she's our teacher at school as well, so you can see how rotten it is anyway, and she goes, 'Tum te tum te tum te tum,' and then says, 'Now, children,' and we have to stand round these daft chairs and stop when the music stops and try and sit on one and there's always a person left over and it's usually me.

Anyway, I win this time and I get a book and it's called *The Little Children's Prayer Book* and Miss Plum says, 'I am pleased to see you've won it, dear. I think you have as much need of it as anybody I know,' and I say, 'Thank you,' and tell our Mam what she said and our Mam says, 'And she's only speaking the truth at that.' Then Miss Plum comes up to our Mam and says, 'I've been wanting to tell you how sorry I was to hear of the death in your family.' Our Mam looks at her and says, 'Oh! Er, well, it's a long time ago now,' and I could see her thinking, death? There's nobody died in our family. Then Miss Plum says, 'It doesn't *seem* very long,' and our Mam says, 'Pardon?' and then Miss Plum tells her how I had told this teacher at school that my granny had died (that was the day old Gorilla Face was going to get me) and I can see our Mam going redder and redder and she just says, 'Yes, well, thank you,' to Miss Plum until Miss Plum goes away and then she grabs hold of my jumper at the back and she says, 'Home, madam.'

Now I'm lying here in rotten old bed with that rotten old book that I won at that rotten old game and our Mam says I've got to recite every single prayer in the rotten old book and not to go downstairs until I can remember at least six without looking at the book once. They're all about making people good, these prayers, and I don't reckon much to them at all.

I never heard of anyone being made good by prayers, not yet I haven't. I said that to our Mam and she said, 'You don't know. There's more goes on than you can see,' but if there is, why am I in bed *again* and why did Miss Plum have to tell our Mam about somebody being dead in the first place?

Every night before I go to sleep our Mam says, 'Say your prayers,' and every night for weeks I've been saying, 'And please can I have those books for Christmas?' Every night our Mam says, 'Now start again because you know you should never ask for anything for yourself,' so I says to our Mam, 'But what's the good of praying if you can't ask for things for yourself?' Our Mam says that's exactly what the good of praying is, but all the same, three books, that wouldn't have been a big thing for God to do, would it? And now because our Mam made me cross out my bit about the books every night, they've gone and got themselves sold.

It's lovely lying in bed on Christmas Eve though. Our Lucy and Rose don't come to bed till late and I lie and think about all the things I'm going to find in the pillow slip in the morning. We put a pillow slip at the bottom of the bed and our Mam ties a big pink bow on mine so that it won't get mixed up with our Lucy's and Rose's.

I look at the candle and it's still only burnt halfway down so I think I'll have a puppet show on the wall and I make all these shadows with my hands and I can do a lovely swan and I think, a white swan in white snow at Christmas, and then I must have fallen asleep because when I look at the candle again, I can't see it on account of it being pitch black in the bedroom.

I shout, 'Mam! Mam!' and our Mam goes, 'Oh dear! Who's that?' I say, 'It's me, Mam,' and she says, 'What's wrong?' and I say, 'There's nothing wrong, it's Christmas Day,' and our Dad goes, 'Oh!' groan, groan, moan, moan – 'Do you know what time it is?' and I say, 'It's Christmas Day,' and he says, 'It's two o'clock. It's too early. Go back to sleep.' So I lie down again and our Lucy kicks me and says, 'Do you know what I wish for Christmas?' and I say, 'No,' and she says, 'That you'd disappear,' and I say, 'Ha, ha,' and our Rose goes, 'Oh!' – sigh, sigh, yawn, yawn – 'Shut up you two and let's go to sleep.'

So I lay there staring into the dark for about four more hours and then I shout our Mam and she says, 'Not again!' Our Dad says, 'It's three o'clock. *Go back to sleep*,' and I lay there for at least another fifteen hours this time and then I shout our Mam and she says, 'If ever a woman suffered!' Our Dad says, 'It's five o'clock. *One more time and Christmas Day will be cancelled!*' so I think, 'Huh! Some Christmas. Everybody getting mad at me before it even starts,' and I lie there and this time I wait till Christmas Day is practically over and then I shout, 'Mam!' and she says 'Dear Heaven!' Our Dad says, 'Oh! ' – groan, groan – 'All right, get up' and he says to our Mam, 'It's only quarter to six, you know,' and our Mam says, 'Well, we might as well all get up now,' and by half-past six, we're all sat downstairs drinking tea and surrounded by presents and paper and happiness.

Except for our Joe. He says, 'You ought to do something about her,' but really I think he's glad to be up as well because he's got a bell for his old bike and a lamp and other stupid things boys get.

I got a pen and pencil set and some games and an orange and an apple and a mouth organ which I was very pleased about because I really wanted a mouth organ and, right at the bottom of the pillow case, there were the books. The whole three books from the paper shop window. I said I was sorry to God about the things I'd thought about prayers and then I opened my books and they are so beautiful that I'm going to keep them in the box with this paper so that nobody touches them and dirties the pages. Nobody goes in my box because it's got *Private – Keep Out* written on it in big black letters and when I showed it our Mam she said, 'Oh yes, that'll keep people out all right.' So that's where my books are going to go. Even our Joe doesn't go in my box because he has one exactly the same and he knows if he goes in mine, then I'll go in his.

I also got a doll – yuk, yuk, yuk. Old Flo bought me this doll and she gives me this big box and she says, 'You make sure you look after it, my lass, else I'll be after you,' and I hadn't even opened the box by then. I thought, oh crikey, whatever it is, Old Flo will be coming round every minute and saying, 'Now then, my lass, are you looking after it?' I opened it and there it was, this doll.

It was as old as anything but its clothes had all been washed. 'It were mine when I was a little lass myself,' Old Flo says. It's not a bad doll. At least it doesn't have big blue eyes and yellow curls like Gloria Hottentot, who I hate very much.

It has eyes that are painted on and they just look at you and she has little pink lips and they only just smile and you can't see any teeth at all. She doesn't have any proper hair, but she has some plaits made out of wool and when you take her bonnet off the plaits come off as well because they're sewn on to the bonnet. I like her.

'What's her name?' I said to Old Flo and she says, 'I expect you'll want to give her a new name?' and I said, 'Oh no. How will she know who she is if she's got a new name?' So Old Flo says, 'Her name is Matilda Virginia Anne.' I say to Old Flo, 'I think that's the nicest name I ever heard in all my life,' and then I says to our Mam, 'Why didn't you call me something nice like Matilda Virginia Anne?' and our Mam says, 'Because you're a little madam and that's always suited you down to the ground,' and so me and Matilda V. A. went upstairs and I'm writing this in my room.

But that's it. I'm not writing any more because I've decided I don't want to be a writer when I grow up after all. I've decided to be a lady boxer instead.

All About Barn Owl Books

If you've ever scoured the bookshops for that book you loved as a child or the one your children wanted to hear again and again and been frustrated then you'll know why Barn Owl Books exists. We are hoping to bring back many of the excellent books that have slipped from publishers' backlists in the last few years.

Barn Owl is devoted entirely to reprinting worthwhile out-of-print children's books. Initially we will not be doing any picture books, purely because of the high costs involved, but any other kind of children's book will be considered. We are always on the lookout for new titles and hope that the public will help by letting us know what their own special favourites are. If anyone would like to photocopy and fill in the form below and give us their suggestions for future titles we would be delighted.

We do hope that you enjoyed this book and will read our other Barn Owl titles.

Books I would like to see back in print include:

____

____

____

____

Signature

____

Address

____

____

Please return to Ann Jungman, Barn Owl Books
15 New Cavendish Street, London W1M 7AL